The demon stepped forward, twirling the pipe like a baton. "What's the matter? The big bad vampire can't take on the little guy from the street?"

"Oh, please," Angel replied.

Angel made a quick move to knock the pipe from the fake Gunn's hand.

The demon turned in an instant, blocking the vampire's kick with its shoulder and arm. The pipe in the demon's other hand connected with Angel's ankle.

Pain shot up Angel's leg. That kind of move might have broken some bones in a human. But that wasn't what worried Angel.

The demon had guessed what Angel was going to do. He had fought side by side with Charles Gunn for more than three years. Gunn knew all his moves. That meant the demon knew his moves as well.

So much, then, for the element of surprise.

Angel™

Available from Pocket Books

ANGEL™

dark mirror

Craig Shaw Gardner

**An original novel based on the television series
created by Joss Whedon & David Greenwalt**

POCKET
BOOKS

New York   London   Toronto   Sydney

Historian's Note: This book takes place in the fourth season of *Angel*.

First Pocket Books edition April 2004
Copyright © 2004 by Twentieth Century Fox Film Corporation.
All Rights Reserved.

Pocket Books
An imprint of Simon & Schuster
Africa House
64–78 Kingsway
London WC1B 6AH
www.simonsays.co.uk

Printed in Great Britain by Cox & Wyman Ltd, Reading, Berkshire

First 10 9 8 7 6 5 4 3 2 1

A CIP catalogue record for this book is available from
the British Library

ISBN 0-7434-8998-5

For the usual suspects—Mary, Victoria, Richard, and Jeff—you know what you did.

PROLOGUE

Let me tell you, it isn't easy looking up and finding *that* walking toward you. If there's one thing you don't want to see, it's your mirror image coming at you with a gun in his hand and murder on his mind. Yeah, your mirror image—except you're in the middle of some bloody alley and there's not a mirror in sight.

I should have listened to Gloria while she was still alive. I hadn't been able to save her; too full of myself, I guess. She had said her twin sister was out to kill her. Except she didn't have a twin sister. And now there were two of me. And one of me was going to end up dead as well, unless I did something quick.

I held up my hand and told the other me to hold it there. The other me kept on coming. He was laughing and waving his gun. Idiot that I am, I had left my own piece in the glove compartment of my

1

Honda. The other me laughed and laughed, as if this were the greatest game in the world.

I'd had enough of the game already. I didn't wait for the other me to get too close. I took off running.

I knew this part of town pretty well. But if that guy with the gun was really just another me, he'd know it too. If he was going to kill me, he'd found the best place to do it quietly. I was in the warehouse district, a maze of streets and alleys and big brick buildings—busy as hell during the week. But it was Sunday. We pretty much had the streets to ourselves.

It only occurred to me then that the whole string of evidence about Gloria, the note, the bloody glove, the phone call cut off midsentence—it had all been a setup to get me right here. And this guy chasing me, who was me and not me all at the same time, had known just how to reel me in.

I kept on running, taking a zigzag course between the buildings. I heard two shots fired, but I was already around a corner. Bits of brick fell on me as another bullet hit above my head. I dove to the other side of a low brick wall, then sprinted inside an open building. A couple of the businesses here stayed open seven days a week. I figured if I could get around other people, I might be a little safer, at least for a minute. Not that I could go to the authorities. What could I tell them: that I was trying to kill myself? I only knew of one place that would even believe me. I had to shake the other me and get over there before he did.

I turned a corner and walked quickly down the empty hallway. My shoes were the only sound on the worn linoleum of the corridor. I pulled the cell phone from my pocket and punched the speed-dial.

"Angel Investigations," a cheery female voice said on the other end.

"Fred?" I replied. "This is Phil Manchester."

"Phil!" She sounded pleasantly surprised. "Have you got any work for us?" I had passed the occasional odd case their way over the past year or so. But I didn't have time for small talk.

"Yeah," I replied, "except this time the case is me." A door slammed somewhere in the building, the noise echoing through the empty corridors. "I'll have to call you back."

I looked up, realizing I had made it all the way to the lobby. This particular aging building sat on the edge of the warehouse district, facing out toward a major thoroughfare. I peered through the dirty glass and wondered if my double was hiding, trying to get off a clear shot. I thought about the noise I'd just heard. If that had been the other me, he was still too far away to do me any harm.

I smiled. Maybe I could get out of here after all. On the other side of the glass, just down the boulevard, was an actual L.A. Transit bus. I pushed my way out of the building and ran toward the stop, waving both arms above my head, knowing that if he didn't stop, I was making one hell of a target. To the driver's credit, he noticed me and pulled over. I quickly climbed the steps, paid my fare, and walked back to join the three other passengers.

The bus quickly left the warehouse district behind.

I'd lost him, at least for the moment. Unless he was in a car, following me. I moved all the way to the back of the bus and tried to get a look out the last, slightly opened window. There was hardly any traffic in this part of town on Sunday, and I didn't see any car that seemed to be taking the bus's route. Besides, following me so openly wasn't the way I would have done it, so I couldn't see my double doing it either. Maybe that was foolish, but what else did I have to go on?

The bus wound its way toward the city center, making the occasional stop along the way. It wasn't the fastest way to get across town. It gave the other me plenty of time to get where I was going. I decided I'd better make the second call.

Fred answered again.

"It's Phil. We need a code word or two."

"Okay," Fred replied cheerfully, as if this were the most normal request in the world.

"Remember the first case I brought to you? The guy who had disappeared in the water filtration plant?"

Fred laughed. "Dan Dinkelman. How could I ever forget?"

"Fine. When I see you next, his name will be the first two words out of my mouth. Tell everybody else. If my first two words are anything else, it isn't me. No matter how much it looks like me."

"Gotcha. Do we get an explanation when you get here?"

"As much of an explanation as I've got."

"Gotcha on that, too."

I looked out the window. We were getting into Central L.A. "I'll be there in half an hour."

"I'll let everybody know. Sounds like we're in for some fun."

I snapped the cell phone shut. "Fun" was not a word I'd use here.

I sat and thought about what I already knew about my doppelgänger.

Gloria had said her double knew everything about her past, up to the moment of the split, and maybe even some things from after that. That was a particularly creepy thought, but I wasn't sure it was true. My guess was that, whatever or whoever these double guys were, they thought pretty much the same way we did—at least up to the point when the two selves split. As if I knew what I was talking about. Exactly how much they knew, and how they knew it—heck, how they even came to be—was a mystery. Now if only I

5

could live long enough to figure them out.

The bus stopped across the street from the Hilton. I jumped out and grabbed a cab. It was time to get to Angel's hotel.

A lot of the local PIs wouldn't work with Angel Investigations. I don't have the luxury of turning down work, and thus sometimes find myself walking the weird end of the street. No one knows weird like the Angel team.

The cabbie pulled up in front of the old hotel that Angel called home. I paid the fare and got out of the car, looking both ways for signs of the other me. It looked clear. I walked quickly across the sidewalk. The hotel's front door opened before I could grab the handle.

"Oh," Fred said, full of nervous energy even more than usual. She jumped out and slammed the door behind her, calling in a loud voice, "It's the *pizza* delivery! Wait a moment. My wallet's here somewhere."

That meant my other self was already here.

"Dan Dinkelman," I replied.

"Hi, Phil," Fred replied in little more than a whisper. "Angel's inside. And so are you. But our guy will grab your guy and maybe we can figure—"

A shout came from across the street. It was Gunn, Fred's coworker, running out of an alley and pointing around the nearby corner.

And there I was, ten steps away, pointing the gun

and smiling. He had slipped out the back door and had come around the side. I probably would have tried the same trick.

"Can't we talk about this?" I asked.

"Not bloody likely," he said as he aimed the piece right between my eyes. He was going to finish this before it got complicated.

After all, it was what I would have done.

CHAPTER ONE

Fred hung up the phone and looked at the two others working in the hotel lobby that served as headquarters for Angel Investigations. Up until the call, it had been one of those waiting-around afternoons that you got in the detective biz—especially their peculiar corner of the detective biz. Angel—your basic man in black—walked into the lobby, fresh from a nap in his room downstairs. "Who was that?"

"Our detective friend Phil," Fred replied.

Cordelia looked up from her filing, one more bit of the exhaustive catch-up she'd been doing after all her many months away. She blew an errant strand of blond hair out of her face. "Oh. Does he have a case for us?"

Fred smiled at that. Trust Cordy to think about the bottom line. "Actually, I think he wants to hire us for himself!"

Cordy shrugged and smiled. "Hey, it's still business."

"But sort of weird business," Fred amended.

"Is there any other kind?" Charles Gunn asked from the corner where he had been polishing weapons. Fred smiled at that, too. Charles could be so funny. Actually, everybody around here could be funny, sometimes, but there was just that way that Charles said things. Everybody around here was special. Cordy had her visions and her organizational skills, Wesley his encyclopedic knowledge of demonkind from his days as a Watcher, Charles his years of fighting vampires on the L.A. streets. And Angel, the vampire with a soul, was the reason all of them were here. Compared with them, what did Winifred Burkle have, besides an extensive knowledge of theoretical physics and a few years' experience trapped in a hell dimension? Fred sighed. She wished she had one half of Charles's fighting skills, one quarter of Wesley's occult education. Heck, she wished she had one tenth of Cordy's fashion sense.

Still, she and Charles had been the ones to get together. She looked back at her dark-skinned Romeo, his handsome, bald head reflected in the double-bladed silver battle-ax he was sharpening. He flashed a smile back at her. Sometimes these wonderful things just happened.

Fred realized it had gotten awfully quiet in there. She glanced away from Charles.

"Oh, my," she whispered.

Both Cordy and Angel had that look in their eyes again. Were she and Charles back to exchanging goofy smiles? Fred could feel her cheeks going crimson. Angel Investigations, Puppy Love Division. If only Charles wasn't so adorable.

Fred cleared her throat. She decided it was a good time to talk about Phil. Or the two Phils. Or at least what the one Phil had told her about the two. . . .

She cleared her throat a second time and quickly relayed what Phil had told her over the phone: "Dan Dinkelman," code word and all.

"Wait a minute," Cordy pointed out. "If this is true, how are we going to tell which one is which?"

"Well, if the wrong one shows up, we'll nab him," Charles replied. "We should be able to handle Phil."

Angel grinned at that. "I don't know. He's pretty wiry."

"Two Phils," Cordy corrected. "Who are out to kill each other."

"So we catch two Phils," Angel agreed. "And get them to tell us which one is real."

"Uh, reality check here," Cordy said. "Isn't each Phil going to insist he's the real one?"

And who around here was really good at reality

10

checks? Fred was surprised she hadn't thought about it sooner. "Lorne would know. We'll just get Phil to sing."

Angel nodded. Charles grinned. Cordy raised her eyebrows. That made sense to all of them. Lorne was a demon who took up residence in the hotel upstairs after Caritas was destroyed by Holtz in a battle with the gang. He was tall, green, had a pair of bright red horns, and was a heck of a nice guy, who just happened to be able to read people's inner beings—but only if they sang a song. Fred bet that Angel and Charles could convince just about anybody to sing. "But if this is real—" she began.

"Phil wouldn't kid around about this sort of thing," Charles agreed.

"This double thing sounds both confusing and dangerous," Angel said. "Who knows what the double is, what it's capable of? The other Phil could be a killing machine."

Cordy shook her head. "Just another day at Angel Investigations."

The door swung open. It was Phil, tall and skinny, wearing his rumpled raincoat and his usual frown. He ran down the steps to the lobby. "Am I the first one here?" were the first words out of his mouth.

Cordy glanced sharply at the others, then smiled in Phil's direction. "What? The first one? Is there going to be a party?"

Phil frowned. "I'm afraid I've got a serious situation here."

"We've got some other business we're finishing up." Angel shrugged, as though this were all beyond his control. "Talk to Cordy. We'll all listen in another minute."

Phil looked a little put out, or maybe like he'd had something bad for lunch. But then Phil always looked like that. But, Fred decided, he looked a little worse than usual, his frown lines a little deeper, his raincoat even more rumpled. Like he'd eaten something bad for two meals in a row.

"I've got a story you're not going to believe," he began as Angel ushered Gunn and Fred into the office, firmly closing the door.

Fred looked through the plate-glass window at Cordy talking with the newcomer. "He didn't say Dan Dinkelman."

"So that means he wasn't the one who called," Charles added. "It could still be Phil."

"We need to get both of them here," Angel said, "and figure it out then. Somebody should wait outside for the other Phil to show."

Charles nodded at that. "It's daylight. I'm on the job."

Angel nodded back. "I'm going to call Wesley in, then go out there and see what I can find."

"What about me?"

Charles and Angel both turned to Fred.

"Somebody's got to wake up Lorne," Angel said in that oh-so-serious tone of his. "Are we ready?"

"I'm on it," Charles said.

Fred sighed. "I guess I'm on it too."

Charles headed toward the back door. Fred smiled as she passed Cordy and the guy who looked like Phil on her way to the stairs. Lorne could be a real party demon—and a little difficult to rouse the following morning. But if Fred knocked loud enough and long enough—like Cordy said, just another day in the glamorous life of Angel Investigations.

Gunn was ready for anything. Almost.

A half hour ago Phil had shown up in the lobby of Angel's hotel. But it could be the wrong Phil. They'd only know after they got both of them together.

So Gunn stood in the alley across from the hotel, waiting for Phil number two. In those daylight hours when a vampire like Angel couldn't venture outdoors, Gunn was the go-to guy, trained on the streets to handle just about anything. *Just about anything.* In situations like these, it mostly meant a lot of waiting. Not that he minded. He supposed it was better than waking up Lorne.

A cab stopped in front of the hotel, and Phil stepped out. He paid the cabbie, then turned to walk to the double front doors.

Gunn leaned against the brick wall that hid him from the street, debating the best way to handle this. He could just grab him from behind. Still, if both these guys were supposed to be the real deal, he didn't imagine either one of them would act very guilty. It would probably be better just to call out his name.

He saw Fred step out of the lobby before Phil could reach the door. Well, that meant Lorne had to be up too.

Winifred Burkle. Her name always made Gunn smile. Her brown hair framed her delicate oval face—a face that looked a little worried at the moment.

Maybe he needed to check this out.

Gunn stepped out of hiding. "Hey, Phil!"

And he realized there were two of them. Two Phils, like two rumpled raincoat mirror images, one just in front of the entrance, another half a block away. They stared at each other as though no one else were there.

"Charles! Look out!" Fred stepped out of the doorway. She pointed at the advancing twin. "I came out here to tell Phil his double was inside. But the other one snuck out the side."

Gunn figured it was time to move before something worse happened.

"Oh no, you don't!" He was on the move now, running toward the Phil who had escaped the hotel, the Phil who was pulling a gun out of his coat. The two Phils shouted at each other. The nearer one wanted to talk; the other said, "Not bloody likely!"

He took off running toward the guy who stood nearer to Fred, who seemed rooted to the spot, staring at his double. *Maybe,* Gunn thought, *I should have armed myself with some sort of weapon too.* The gift of hindsight. He'd never really thought he'd have a problem with someone like Phil.

But the guy with the gun was having trouble slowing down, and Gunn used his own momentum to push away from the ground and hit him with a flying kick. The .45 in his hand went off, the gunshot echoing down the street. The second Phil cried in pain.

But the first Phil staggered back, knocked off-balance by Gunn's attack. Gunn used the back of his fist to knock the .45 out of his hand.

Gunn spun around as Fred ran into the street. The second Phil clutched at his side, a dark brown spot spreading on his raincoat. He staggered over to the .45 Gunn had knocked away from his twin.

"Phil!" Gunn shouted. "No!"

But the wounded Phil staggered forward. "You don't understand. If I don't kill him now, he's bound to kill me. And that's only the start of their plan!"

Gunn didn't want anyone dying there. He scooped up the fallen .45 before the other man could get it, pointing it right at the nearer Phil's chest. "Don't make me do it, man."

But the man Gunn had taken out was on his feet again, and running. And he was heading straight for Fred. "Charles!" she yelled as the first Phil grabbed her.

Gunn swung the piece around. "Get away from her!"

But the man had turned Fred around to face him. He opened his mouth, and a glittering mist spread out from between his lips to cover her face.

The demon pulled her closer. Gunn didn't know what it was trying to do to Fred. He just wanted to make it stop.

Fred cried out in panic, managing to push her attacker back a couple of steps. Gunn saw his opening. He pulled the trigger.

The bullet caught the Phil-creature in the shoulder. It shrieked, a sound halfway between air rushing from a balloon and the grinding of metal gears. The Phil-thing fell to the ground, its skin bubbling up where it was exposed, rippling beneath the raincoat. The bubbles turned a deep green, bursting one after another, eating through the raincoat with a sizzling sound. In less than a minute the thing was gone, leaving only a dark puddle where its demise had pockmarked the asphalt.

Gunn looked at Fred, who was staring at the spot where the false Phil had melted. "Are you all right?" he called.

"I think so." She waved past Gunn. "Phil needs help."

Gunn turned around. The real Phil was bleeding heavily from his side. Fred had barely missed getting hurt. And Phil had said these things were only getting started.

Gunn guessed his waiting days were over.

17

CHAPTER TWO

Fred couldn't stop shivering.

She didn't realize how much the whole thing had shaken her up until she had gotten into the ambulance. She had stood over the bleeding Phil—the real, human, dying Phil—while Cordy quickly called 911. The ambulance arrived a minute later. The police were right on their tail. Charles fielded their questions. She heard him tell a story that was true, after a fashion, about how Phil had told them he was in trouble and had been shot by an unknown assailant, who had then fled. The gun was still on the pavement. No one had touched it. Charles made no mention of demonic doubles. You don't talk magic with the authorities.

They had gotten the real Phil stabilized. He wasn't in any immediate danger. The EMTs asked if anybody wanted to accompany the victim. Fred volunteered. She had had enough of standing around. And she wanted to do something for Phil. Maybe it was all nervous energy, but she couldn't let her connection with this guy end here. He had come to them for help, and they had been too slow. They had failed him, and nobody at Angel Investigations ever liked to fail.

But he was still alive. With a little luck he would recover and be able to tell them what was really going on. Then they could understand whatever had tried to kill Phil, and they could keep the world safe from this latest demonic threat. That was another reason to keep close.

The cops nodded. She could go. She had a moment while the EMTs secured the patient, so she quickly went to her room to grab a book and a couple of personal things. The cops watched her as she climbed into the ambulance.

That was a given: The few times that Angel Investigations had had to deal directly with the authorities, the police had always been suspicious. She supposed that was the cops' job. They were probably just as suspicious of all the normal private investigators in the city. Maybe even more so. Most of the cases handled by Angel Investigations were outside the cops' usual jurisdiction. Heck, A.I. covered the occasional divorce or missing person's case—it just so happened that all their divorces had something to do with monsters and vampires.

The EMTs let her ride up front in the shotgun seat. She looked out the front window, the siren wailing, the traffic parting like the Red Sea in front of Charlton Heston in *The Ten Commandments*. Under other circumstances, it would have been a great ride. But she kept worrying about Phil.

He was one of the few locals they had really connected with in the four years Angel Investigations had been working out of L.A. They lived in one of the biggest cities in the world, yet because of the nature of their business, they kept mostly to themselves, only associating with a very few who understood where they were coming from—who understood about the hidden Los Angeles, the dark side of sunny California, full of creatures ready to drink your blood or steal your soul . . . or far, far worse. You didn't have time for many friends when you spent every waking moment saving the world.

At least, for a while there, the crew at Angel Investigations had one another. But now their tightly knit group was unraveling at the edges. Wesley and the gang were learning to trust one another again—it was a wonder they were talking at all, after that business with Angel's son—and Cordelia wasn't herself yet. Fred supposed a long stay on the astral plane could do that to a person. And then there was Connor, Angel's son, who had been kidnapped as an infant and forced to grow up in a hell dimension—and who had been taught that Angel was to blame.

Fred sighed. It was such a sad story. At least Connor had found a place to stay, and seemed to have declared a sort of truce for the time being with Angel and the others. And she and Charles were still together, thank goodness, but she sometimes wondered if even their relationship could hold up in the face of the madness they lived every day.

She shuddered again, thinking about what had happened back there on the street.

It had looked so much like Phil. Maybe that's what got to her about the double—the demon could have copied *any* one of them. This twin thing gave her the creeps.

But why was this making her so upset? Since she had joined Angel Investigations, she had faced it all—and had managed to come out of it with no more than the occasional bruise. Not to mention the fact that she had survived falling into a dimension of demons. Sure, she had mostly hidden, but she *had* survived—until Angel and company managed to rescue her. And yet, this threat felt so personal.

She could still see the demon's eyes, staring into her own. The false Phil had grabbed her for a moment. It had pushed its face forward, nose to nose, so close that she could smell its breath. It was not a human smell. The odor was nearly over-powering, both sweet and foul at the same time. It made Fred think of rotten fruit.

And then he was gone. Nothing happened—except for that weird mist that had settled around her—yet she felt violated. It all had to do with "personal space," she supposed. That, and being breathed on by a demon.

The shivering was back. And this time it didn't want to stop.

She faced death two to three times a week. She had survived a world of demons. This shouldn't be affecting her this way.

"Can we help you, miss?" the EMT called from the back.

"N-no," Fred managed. "I'll be fine."

The driver glanced over for an instant. "What's happening?"

"She can't stop shaking," the other fellow replied. He turned back to Fred. "It's nothing to be ashamed of. We see this reaction a lot. It's sort of a post-traumatic stress disorder. Violence gets to people."

"I guess it does," Fred agreed.

"We've got an extra blanket here, miss."

"Thanks. I'll be okay."

The EMT held out a thick, blue blanket. "Sure you will, miss. Sure you will."

She took the blanket. The EMT helped drape it

over her shoulders. It *did* help. The shivering slowed to a tremble.

"We can get someone to meet us at the hospital," the EMT continued. "Is there anyone you would like us to call?"

"I'll be okay," she said again. The EMTs nodded and left her alone. She would call the hotel later, once she got some idea of Phil's condition.

Fred closed her eyes.

She had offered to accompany Phil to the hospital. *I saw him bleeding on the ground.* She couldn't do anything else. *I saw the other's face, the demon's face, pressed close to my own.* She'd stay with Phil until she got some answers.

"I'll be fine," she said, more to herself than to the others.

Somebody had to care.

Lorne looked out the window, at the darkening Los Angeles street. They had woken him up, just in time to miss all the action. From what they told him of the crime scene, he decided it had been a good day to sleep in. But there was a definite down vibe happening in this hotel. Gunn was working on the weapons, Cordy was deep into the computer, and Angel was back in the office, doing whatever he did back there. Advanced brooding, most likely. Fred had been gone for a couple hours now. And none of them were talking. Lorne didn't need any

23

of them to sing to know they were all blaming themselves.

Angel and his cronies wanted to save everybody —real hero types. Phil Manchester had been shot. There was a possibility he wouldn't survive. They realized they had let an associate down—and sure, you could make excuses about facing an unknown menace and the element of surprise. Except that the folks around here didn't believe in excuses.

That was one of the reasons Lorne stuck around this place. If L.A. was ever going to become the real sunshine capital, it would start in someplace like this hotel, with its odd mix of mortal and immortal with one thing in common: They really cared about their fellow beings, and were crazy enough to do something about them. Lorne sighed. Just call him an old softy.

Lorne frowned. He thought he saw somebody moving out in the twilight, just the other side of that hedge by the entryway. This hotel wasn't exactly in the most populated corner of town, no doubt one of the reasons the original establishment had gone out of business. During the day there was a fair amount of vehicular traffic and a modest amount of foot traffic, but at night they saw fewer passersby than your average ghost town.

Lorne squinted. Yes, someone was in the shadows. Somebody was watching the place. Some skinny guy in a trench coat with a bad haircut. Somebody who looked a little bit like Phil.

Lorne stepped away from the window. "Uh, guys?"

Gunn looked up. "Yeah?"

"I think we have company."

"I'll go take a look."

Gunn grabbed a medieval mace—the nearest weapon at hand—and strode out the front door.

"Over by the hedge!" Lorne called after him. Gunn moved quickly in that direction. Lorne stood by the window, looking for any further sign of the man in the coat.

Gunn came back two minutes later, shaking his head. "Nobody. Just as empty out there as usual."

Lorne frowned. "I could have sworn I saw something moving."

"Probably just another breeze," Gunn replied.

"Or a small earthquake," Cordelia added, not looking up from her computer. "We're just about due."

Had it been Lorne's imagination? Maybe he had to lay off all those exotic concoctions he'd consumed last night, especially the ones with recipes from other dimensions. Or maybe it had been the pepperoni pizza he'd had after the drinks.

Or maybe Gunn scared whoever it was off for the moment, but there really was somebody watching them.

Connor felt like he was a stranger everywhere. The adults told him stories that contradicted each other. The man Connor had called Father had taught him to hate the vampire Angel. And yet Angel—who claimed to be his real father—and his friends had been nothing but kind to him. And Connor did have certain talents that were above and beyond those of most people he had known—certainly beyond the man who had raised him—talents like the strength and speed of a vampire.

Connor no longer knew what to believe. He needed some time to himself. He had found this loft in an abandoned building, cleaned it up, and brought in some furniture he had scavenged from the streets. He needed a place he could call his own.

He thought about those who surrounded Angel. Fred, Gunn, and Wesley had always treated Connor well. Heck, Cordelia always made him smile. And that demon Lorne seemed a lot nicer than most of the monsters Connor used to kill every day just to stay alive. Some of them seemed to have their problems with Angel, too, but they kept on working with him. Why?

He wished his father were still around. Answers had always been easy with him. Even if, Connor guessed, sometimes they were the wrong answers.

He looked down and saw somebody standing directly beneath the neighborhood's one working streetlight, and she was looking up at him. A well-dressed blond woman, old enough to be his mother.

This was a rough neighborhood. Connor could handle anything that went down around here, but a classy lady like that—why was she standing out there, watching him?

Alarms went off in Connor's head. He had grown up in a place where danger was everywhere and every minute, and this looked like another danger—a rich woman, a target, unable to defend herself in a place like this. Sort of like a pretty flower that hid a plant waiting to eat you whole.

Maybe she was there just to lure him out. She made no attempt to move away from the streetlight or try to come inside.

Was this some new trick from Angel? Or did she come here for some other reason? Could she be an old associate of his father's, come to talk to him?

She waved.

Connor backed away from the window. He stopped breathing for a minute, listening for any other movement in the building, the sounds of feet on stairs, the creak of boards, the squeak of hinges. Nothing. He was still alone.

For now, he would stay put. Maybe he could get Cordy to help him figure out who was watching. Maybe he did need more than just himself, sometimes.

He just wanted someplace safe, someplace to call home.

Angel always hated this part—the part where they had encountered some unknown creature, obviously a threat, but otherwise a total mystery. How did you defeat the unknown? Sometimes, you could chop off their heads, but other times, the body would grow a new head and the head a new body, and you'd have two creatures for the price of one. He needed to know a bit more about this new doppelgänger before he went any further. He needed a plan of action. Then, like usual, he could save the world.

But his team wasn't quite in world-saving mode. Gunn was still handling the police. Fred had gone to the hospital to keep an eye on Phil. Cordy was still getting used to being human again. And Lorne, well, he was a great demon and all, and really useful in many situations, but he needed to be given direction.

Angel had to face it: They needed Wesley at times like this. "Cordy?" he said.

"I hope you don't mind," she said with that sweet smile. How could he mind with a smile like that? "I've already called Wesley. He said he's got some ideas. He'll bring over a couple books."

Gunn pushed open the front door. "They finally left! For now, at least." He scowled and urged his voice an octave lower. "'We may have further questions for you and your company, Mr. Gunn.'" He shook his head as he walked down the stairs into the main lobby. "We'll be seeing them again."

Lorne looked up from the magazine he was reading. "Do the cops have any reason to suspect us?"

Gunn shrugged. "I did a couple things back in my vampire-hunting youth that are probably still on file. Nothing ever came to real charges, though."

"Wasn't Fred listed as a missing person?" Lorne asked. "When I had my club, I used to pay off some guys just to keep the cops away."

"Last time I was in trouble around here . . . ," Angel mused. "Well, they don't keep records that far back."

"But that wasn't really you," Cordy pointed out.

"You mean because I was Angelus?" he asked, using the name he had preferred in his truly evil days, before the gypsies had restored his soul. "I've still got Angelus in me. He's never very far away."

Cordy shook her head. "And I've just spent far too much time on a vacation with the higher powers! We've all got skeletons in our closets around here."

"And the people around here have some pretty fancy closets," Lorne agreed.

Angel had another thought. "I bet the cops are

after us because they don't hear from us. Most private investigators are probably pestering the police all the time, sniffing for clues on their investigations."

Gunn picked up on it. "But we don't exactly go into typical law enforcement territory."

"So when we *do* show up on their radar, the cops stick to us like a fly on yesterday's dinner," Lorne finished the thought.

"Exactly," Angel agreed. "So we're going to have to be doubly careful in handling this particular demon."

"If the demon doesn't end up handling us," Lorne added. "What? From what you said about that demon, it could be making a copy of any one of us. The thing was out there on the street with Gunn. And what it did to Fred was downright creepy."

Gunn nodded at that. "Yeah, that thing got much too close to my girl."

"We don't know yet what it takes to make these doubles," Angel pointed out.

"Maybe all they need is to get close," Lorne added. "I tell you, some of the strange creatures who walked into my bar . . ." He let the rest of the sentence hang, as if it might be better to not give detailed descriptions.

Angel was starting to wish that Wesley would hurry up. They needed to know something about these doppelgängers before they went up against them. What if hurting the demon double also harmed the original? Stranger things had happened since he had come to L.A. They needed something to enable them to form a plan of attack.

"So what you're saying is that we can't trust anybody," Gunn said.

Cordy shook her head. "Business as usual at Angel Investigations."

Angel looked up as he heard a bang against the front door. That would be their exiled associate carrying an armload of books, and maybe some explanations.

But it wasn't Wesley. It was Fred. And she looked worn out. Her clothes were rumpled, her hair wasn't combed. Not surprising, Angel realized, considering the close encounter she'd had with a demon only hours ago. Now it looked like that close call was having some long-term effects.

"Fred?" Gunn said. "What happened?"

She tromped down the stairs and made a beeline straight for her beau.

"Fred?" Gunn said again.

She pressed up close to Gunn, putting her arms around him. "I missed you, Charles. I've been through a lot today."

Her exhaustion seemed to cut into her usual reserve. She wasn't usually this demonstrative in public. Even Gunn appeared a little startled by her attention. He took a step back as she pressed her whole weight against him.

She looked to the others, as though only now realizing the rest of them were there.

"The hospital was a total bust. They have guards on top of the guards. They wouldn't even let me near him until he had been 'interviewed by the authorities.'"

She looked back to Gunn. "What could I do? I left our number at the nursing station. They said they'd call as soon as they interviewed him."

"Did Phil say anything in the ambulance?" Angel asked.

"No." She shook her head and stared at the floor. "He had passed out by the time I got to see him. And then they wouldn't let me near him again. Like I said, it was total security. And I'm totally exhausted."

Maybe it was her exhaustion, but it seemed like Fred had given up more easily than usual. Angel wasn't comfortable in leaving this alone.

"Are you feeling some sort of . . . aftereffects of what happened today?" Angel asked.

"What?" Fred hesitated, as if she couldn't figure out what Angel meant. "Oh. You mean that creepy-crawly that grabbed me? No. I'm just a little tired. I think I'll go up to my room."

Lorne strolled across the room to place himself in her path. "Poor Fred." He smiled at the whole group. "Maybe a nice, relaxing sing-along would be in order."

So Angel wasn't the only one to sense something a little strange here.

Fred only stared back at the green-skinned demon.

Lorne shrugged as if his suggestion were an everyday occurrence. "It always helps me."

"I'll do whatever you want, after I take my nap." She stepped past the demon. "Charles?" she called over her shoulder. "Could you come up in a little while?"

"Sure." Gunn's smile looked a little sickly. "I'll be up as soon as we finish down here."

"I'll try to stay awake for you."

They watched in silence as she climbed the stairs.

"She's just tired—right?" Gunn asked the others.

"Alarm bells," Lorne said after she had disappeared on the upstairs landing.

"Like she's been through a close encounter of the worst kind." Cordy stared up the stairs. "It could be her. Not a demon, I mean. We all have bad days. And, in this business, most of us have had *really* bad days."

"I think this could be worse than bad," Gunn replied. "Even *really* bad. What do we do?"

"Well, that's our problem, isn't it?" It was also, Angel realized, the reason he'd probably hesitated, rather than confronted the doppelgänger. "We're not absolutely sure who just went upstairs. We also don't know exactly what the connection is between the double and the original, and—if this isn't Fred—we don't know what this thing can do if it's provoked."

"Maybe we should try to talk to her," Gunn suggested. "Perhaps it is just a really bad day, and we've got no more than a grumpy coworker."

Lorne looked skeptical. "Or maybe not."

Angel nodded. "Whatever happens, this time we have to be ready for an attack. But I don't want us to kill our visitor unless we have to. Maybe we'll need to lock her—or it—in the room until Wesley shows up and we can figure out what to do."

"But why would the thing come here?" Cordy asked. "And why go up to her room?"

Angel thought he had that angle figured. "I have a feeling the demon wants to get each one of us alone."

"Euwww." Cordy made a face. "I don't even want to know where that's going."

Angel hoped they could stop this before it got anywhere near that far. But how? Would they have to question everybody who left the group for even a few minutes?

The phone rang. Cordy answered it, a surprised look on her face. She took the phone away from her ear and looked at the others. "It's Fred. She's at the hospital. They're letting her stay there until Phil wakes up."

Gunn swore under his breath. Both of his hands clenched into fists. He grew very still, almost too calm considering a demon was impersonating the woman he loved.

"We've got to destroy that thing," he said quietly.

"After we ask it some questions," Angel replied. "Grab something to defend yourself." He turned to look up the stairway where the demon had disappeared. "It's time we got to work."

CHAPTER THREE

He supposed he most wanted to be useful.

Wesley Wyndam-Pryce, former member of the Watchers Council, professional demon hunter, and still somewhat disgraced associate of Angel Investigations, had lost his way. They all had, he supposed, with what had happened over the past months. But he had fouled up spectacularly trying to save Angel's son, Connor, from a threat that had never materialized. He had been fooled, really, into betraying Angel and the rest of his friends, and then was almost killed by those who had led him astray.

His life had hit bottom. And then he had started putting it back together again—rescuing Angel after he had figured out what their enemies had done. Then he had found himself called in by his old mates on a couple of their more difficult cases. Not that all was forgiven. There was a distance between them now, a reserve that hadn't been there before. Perhaps the trust they shared in the past could never be completely restored.

Wesley was amazed they had let him back in at all. Well, that which does not kill you makes you strong, he supposed. Or some such nonsense.

The bottom line at Angel Investigations was the conviction that fighting evil was too much for any one individual. Past experience had shown that they were all necessary to the team. When their enemies had pulled them apart, they had almost perished, but together, somehow, they had survived, even triumphed.

Or so Wesley hoped. At the very least, they had called him in once more. Today, he was working, doing what he did best. For now, that would have to be enough.

"That'll be twelve eighty-five."

The cab driver's voice cut through his reverie.

"Certainly," he said as he gathered his things and opened the door. He handed the cabbie fifteen and told him to keep the change. He stepped onto the curb, shifting the heavy books in his arms. Time to make himself useful once more.

He pushed his way through the heavy doors that led inside. Cordelia and Lorne were sitting in the lobby.

"I got here as quickly as I could," he called down to them.

Cordy gave him an apologetic smile. "I'm afraid they've already gone upstairs."

"Pardon?"

"We appear to have a demon infestation," Lorne explained. "A demon infestation that looks like Fred."

Wesley quickly descended the entry stairs down to the main part of the lobby. "Do you think I should join them?"

Cordy and Lorne looked at each other before they answered.

"They'll call us if they need us."

"That's what they said. Direct orders from the boss."

The books felt like dead weight in Wesley's hands. He sighed very softly. "Very well. Tell me everything you know about this creature. Perhaps we may discover its true nature by the time Angel and Gunn have concluded their business."

He would be useful, one way or another.

Gunn didn't like this one bit. Long ago, he had decided he would follow Angel into hell itself if it would save one innocent soul. And they had fought legions of demons, armies of vampires, a hundred different kinds of evil.

But he had never had to take out a demon who looked like the woman he loved.

"You're the one who got a good look at this

creature," Angel whispered. They stood at the end of the hall, twenty feet away from the room. Fred's room. His room. The room that held a demon.

"Is there anything else you can remember about it?" Angel asked.

It? Gunn thought. The demon, not Fred. Maybe talking about *it* would help him focus.

"I was the one who saw both Phils," Gunn replied softly. "They looked exactly alike, at least at first. But that changed after the guns came out. The real Phil got shot, but he just looked like a guy in pain. The other one, the one that grabbed Fred, that guy's face didn't look human at all."

"What do you mean?"

Gunn thought for a minute, shifting the ax from his right hand to his left. "His face, when he grabbed Fred. It twisted up, showing the demon inside. Real ugly stuff. Sort of like you turning into a vamp." He shrugged. "No offense."

"None taken," Angel agreed.

Gunn nodded. "Yeah, I could see the demon face, and it looked made out of rock. And then the thing opened its mouth and shot something out."

"Something?"

"When it grabbed Fred, I could have sworn I saw something pass between them. Something that glittered in the light when it touched Fred's face. Then it was gone. It was like the demon breathed it right back in." Gunn shook his head in disgust.

"So we don't let the thing breathe on us, right?" Angel nodded at the door at the end of the hall. "Besides that, we're going in."

They crept to the door. Gunn heard a soft groan in the distance. It was an old hotel—haunted, before they killed a demon that was feeding off of it. The place still liked to make noises, though; probably wind pushing through the aging timbers, or the foundation sinking into the Los Angeles soil.

Angel raised his hand, listening for movement from the room beyond. They heard nothing. Now, even the building was still.

Gunn grimaced. He'd had enough of demons stealing the face of the woman he loved. "Hell, I'm going in."

The door was unlocked. Gunn pushed it open easily. "Whoa," he said softly.

Angel took a step forward to look over his shoulder.

The room beyond had been torn apart. The mattress hung half off the bed, the bottom sheet torn. The bedclothes and pillows had been flung in a heap by the bathroom.

"This is definitely not like Fred," Gunn said.

Angel stepped to the other side of the room and checked the closet. Gunn squatted sideways to look under the bed. The windows were closed. It was a thirty-foot drop to the street below. Could the demon have left that way? Gunn supposed anything was possible.

The place was a disaster, but Fred—or Fred's double—was nowhere to be seen.

"Maybe the creature was looking for something," Gunn ventured.

"Either that, or this demon is really, really angry," Angel added.

"That too." Gunn nodded.

"But this could be important," Angel continued, waving at the chaos before them. "We know the first demon looked and sounded like Phil. We can also assume he shared some of Phil's memories. We could guess, then, that this demon knows much of what Fred knows."

"Who we are, where we live, who we sleep with." It was Gunn's turn to nod. "She knew her way to the room."

"Yeah, but apparently she didn't know her way to exactly what she was looking for. Something— some notes, maybe, from a project Fred was working on—that would have been in the room when the demon first 'copied' Fred."

"I see what you mean," Gunn replied. "And then—in the time after the demon copy was made—the real Fred came back to the room and either took or moved the things the demon was looking for. Means this creature can maybe steal Fred's memories, but it can't read Fred's thoughts."

Angel nodded. "Yeah, that's a break. I always hate those guys who can read your thoughts."

"So no Fred. So much for the word of a demon." Gunn shrugged, trying to make light of it. "Where now?"

Their answer was a scream. Not a building noise this time. A real, high-pitched, human shriek.

Angel frowned. "That doesn't sound good."

"Was it Cordy?" Gunn asked. He looked even more worried. "It couldn't be Fred?"

"It could even be Lorne," Angel said. The demon had a particularly high, clear, singing voice. Who knew what his screaming voice sounded like? He moved quickly out of the room and to the end of the hall by the staircase, glancing over his shoulder as he ran. "Everything okay down there?"

"You're talking about the scream?" Lorne called up the stairs. "We thought it came from someplace up there."

"It sounded close, though," Cordy added. "Somebody's in trouble."

"Or somebody wants our attention," Gunn said softly.

"Well, they certainly got it," Angel agreed. "Sounds like the thing is hiding somewhere on this floor."

"Hiding, but screaming?" Gunn pointed out. "Hey, maybe they could start shouting, 'This is a trap!'"

"Angel?" Cordy called. "Wesley's down here too."

"Tell him to wait there. And to watch for anything coming from either inside or outside."

Gunn could see Angel's logic. Whereas both Cordy and Lorne could defend themselves in a pinch, Wesley was a highly trained fighter. He could protect all of them from demon attack.

"And as far as this trap business goes," Angel said, "this is our hotel. We know every inch of it. Maybe we can turn the trap around. Gunn, you check out the left hall. I'll head down the other one. If you see or hear anything, give a yell. I don't think this is something either of us wants to be facing alone."

Gunn nodded and headed down the hall. He held the ax now with both hands.

"Remember," Angel called over his shoulder, "the minute you see anything suspicious—shout."

But Gunn had other things on his mind, like how exactly he was going to put an ax through somebody who looked just like Fred.

It could have been much worse. Or so the nurse had said. The bullet had gone straight through Phil. They were still examining the X-rays to make sure it hadn't damaged any vital organs. She hoped everything was all right back at the hotel.

She looked at her watch. She'd been here for hours now. She wondered if she should call the hotel again. Cordy had sounded so strange the last time she'd talked to her—insisting that Fred stay at the hospital. It had felt as though Cordy and the others were hiding something from her.

But why would they do that? All this waiting was making her paranoid. They'd call her cell if they needed her, wouldn't they?

And then there was that envelope Phil had sent her, the one she had brought with her at the last minute. It contained a list of names under the heading TAKEN. Three of the names had been crossed out and replaced by others. The last name he had written was Phil Manchester.

Phil had sent it to the hotel only the day before, addressed specifically to her. She had fetched it from her room before the ambulance ride, thinking maybe she could get Phil to explain.

"Miss? Are you Fred?"

She looked up at a different nurse. "That's me."

"Mr. Manchester is asking for you." She led Fred from the waiting area, past the nursing station, to a small cubicle with a curtain to give the patient privacy. Phil was in there, propped up in a hospital bed. They had cut away his shirt, but most of his skinny chest was covered by a very large bandage.

"Hey, Phil."

"Hey, Fred." His voice was hoarse, barely a whisper.

"I'll give you two a moment alone," the nurse

announced. "Call if you need anything." She pulled the curtain closed behind her.

"Fred," Phil said with a grimace, as though it hurt him to talk. "I'm sorry to drag you into this."

Fred grinned at him. "I wanted to make sure you got here in one piece. We PI types have to stick together."

Phil tried to raise his hand, probably to make some "you shouldn't have" gesture. He didn't have the strength.

The smile faded from her face. "Are you in pain?"

"Maybe. They have me doped up on so much stuff, I don't really know." He made a sound halfway between a laugh and a cough. "They're surprised I'm still awake. I don't think I'm going to stay awake for long." As if to prove his point, the PI's eyes began to close.

"So you wanted to tell me something?" Fred prompted, hoping to gain some information before he drifted off.

Phil grimaced. "I guess you wouldn't know. Not yet. That thing that looked like me"—he took a ragged breath—"it touched you, didn't it?"

"Worse than that, it breathed on me." Fred shivered at the thought.

"Yeah, that's when they get you. I think they steal a little piece of your soul." His eyes closed again.

"Phil?" Fred urged.

Phil opened his eyes, his face a mix of fatigue and pain. "It's why I sent you that list. I know more about this than I ever wanted to. Have seen them destroy three people. You have to kill it before it kills you. Otherwise . . . otherwise . . ." His eyes slid shut again. "You're history."

Fred realized what he was saying. "Then I'm going to have a double? A demon that looks like me? Phil?"

Phil began to snore.

The nurse stuck her head back in the room. "I think he needs to sleep now." She fixed her smile firmly on Fred, an expression that said it was time for her to leave. "It's the best thing for him."

Fred nodded and stepped out of the cubicle.

"Is Mr. Manchester family?" the nurse asked.

Fred paused a second to choose the most prudent answer. "He's a business associate of mine, actually."

She paused a minute, then added, "I was there when he was shot, but I don't know who did it. What if the shooter comes back?"

The nurse's smile softened. "I wouldn't worry. We have a police detail here at night, and security cameras on every floor. I can't think of many places your friend would be safer."

That was it, then. If Phil was safe here, she needed to get back home. She had to tell Wesley what she had learned. And if Phil was right, she had an appointment with a demon that looked like her.

She shivered, thinking of another time and place—the demon world she had been sucked within, until Angel and his fellows had rescued her. It had taken all she had on that other world to hide and to survive.

But this was a different world, and Fred was a different woman. Gunn and Angel, Wesley and Cordy—each had in their own way shown her that she could make a difference. And that she didn't have to hide.

Her life was better now. She didn't want to lose this new life for anything. Especially to some rock-faced demon with glittery slime for breath.

She walked out of the hospital. She had a job to do.

CHAPTER FOUR

Phil Manchester couldn't wake up.

Yet he could smell the sharp tang of antiseptic, hear people's voices drift by in conversation, even feel hands moving his body. But it all felt very, very far away.

He thought he was in the hospital. Sometimes he was aware of conversations. Sometimes they were even about him.

"Mr. Manchester appears to be stable." "He's out of immediate danger." "He'll wake up soon, won't he?" "Only time will tell." "We can't determine the cause." "We'll run some more tests." "He'll wake up soon, won't he?" "Sometimes they do, sometimes they don't." "His shooting is still an active investigation." "We'll keep a man posted."

That would be the cops. So they'd have somebody nearby. He hoped it was somebody he knew, somebody who liked him, not one of the hard-noses he had managed to piss off.

"He'll wake up soon, won't he?"

Sometimes he wasn't even close to awake. Sometimes he dreamed.

He had two different dreams. One was about the investigation that had brought him here. That woman, Gloria. She was a looker, a real Hollywood type. Maybe forty, maybe older—with all the stuff they could do these days, how could you tell?

She had come to him with a story. Her boss wasn't really her boss. He was acting strangely, meeting with people in the middle of the night. Her own life felt threatened.

In Phil's line of work, he met his fair share of nutcases. And he ran across a lot more who weren't telling him the whole story. This case felt more like the second scenario. Gloria and her boss sounded a little bit too close for the typical employer and employee. He bet there were far more than the two of them involved, and he'd run across a jealous spouse and vengeful lover or two in no time flat.

So he had Gloria pay him a small retainer, just to make sure she was serious. And he went to look up the boss, but found two Glorias instead.

What happened next was lost in his dreams.

Sometimes he and Gloria made love. Sometimes, the Gloria he made love to wasn't even human. Sometimes the people he was with—

Gloria, Gloria's boss, even strangers on the street—
would shift their shape, and he would be looking at
himself, another Phil Manchester. But when he
looked down at his hands, he saw they were made
of stone.

The second dream was worse. He saw flashes of
images, places all over L.A., as if he had never been
shot and was still out there, working on the street.

Sometimes he was in a warehouse with others
that looked human but really weren't. Gloria was
there, and her boss was there too. Some of the others looked vaguely familiar, like they were small-
time TV stars or local politicians. But all of them
were working together on something, plotting in
voices and words Phil couldn't understand.

And then he was back on the street again.

Most of the time, he was watching the hotel that
housed Angel Investigations.

In those moments, he thought he could see
through the eyes of the double who had taken over
his life.

And the creature's hands really were made of
stone.

"He'll wake up soon, won't he?"

Detective Grady Small was much, much bigger
than his name. Well over six feet tall, close to 250
pounds, and not too much of that fat, even now.
When he was still on the force, he'd make little

jokes about his name, especially when he'd helped along his private interrogations with his ham-sized fists. It had been nice to see how cooperative the perps could be when they could no longer breathe.

But that was past history. He'd bent and broken too many rules. It was a changed police force now in the City of Angels. The new commissioner believed in doing things in the open, on the up and up. You hurt somebody—let alone kill them—in the course of an investigation, it was your ass that was put on the line. Small put in close to his twenty years. They gave him a little extra credit and pushed him out of the way. Full pension, though. And he was young enough to do some detective work—even some bodyguard gigs. Now it looked like he was going to see some real money. He still had a lot of friends in high places. Now he was going to get what he was owed. What he really deserved.

When Wolfram & Hart called, they said it was something special. Potentially long term.

Small had done the law firm some favors while he was still a cop, and they had repaid him by giving him a couple of small jobs since his retirement. Some of the boys back on the force had second thoughts about working for Wolfram & Hart. There were rumors about shady associations that weren't quite legal, and more than a few unsolved cases that led right to the law firm's heavily guarded door. But to Small, a buck was a buck, and Wolfram & Hart had a lot of bucks.

He'd do just about anything they asked, so long as he got paid.

He drove down to the private underground parking lot. The uniformed attendant frowned at his Buick LaSabre until he told the guy whom he had the appointment with. The attendant was all smiles, then, directing Small to the best place to park, and the quickest way to get through the massive Wolfram & Hart building to keep his appointment.

In the past, the firm had always contacted him in some neutral place—either a bar or a diner that Small liked to frequent. They seemed to know exactly where to find him at any time of day. And the dossiers on the people they wanted him to track down were equally complete—where they lived, when they went to work, when they went to lunch, what they had for lunch. He was able to find both the cases they gave him in a matter of hours; served both sets of papers with hardly any effort. He wondered if the law firm had that kind of information on him as well. Sometimes he wondered if Wolfram & Hart knew everything about everybody.

Not that they would use it against him. Grady Small grinned at the idea. He was too valuable for that. They just wanted to keep him in line. He could respect that.

He pulled the LaSabre into one of three unoccupied spaces marked VISITOR. He locked the car out of habit. The old Buick was probably safer here than in Fort Knox. He had noticed three security cameras as he had driven to his space, and saw a fourth just above the door leading inside. The door slid aside as he approached. He stepped through the opening into a space surrounded by a metal screening device, somewhat larger and more elaborate than the kind they had in public buildings around town. He had expected this kind of security. The man who made the appointment told Small not to bring his gun.

Small took a step forward out of the gate.

A guard with a handgun poking out of a very conspicuous shoulder holster frowned at him. "Sorry. Could you step back, sir?"

Small did as he was told. "I thought you could tell I wasn't carrying."

"That, we know. This machine tells us more than that. It can identify who you are—and what you are. But it can take a moment." The guard's frown softened into more of a neutral position. Probably the closest Small would see to a look of apology.

The guard looked at a computer monitor before him. "You are Grady Small?"

"Yeah, that's me. I've got an appointment—"

"Down to the end of this hall," the guard cut him off. "Take the elevator one floor up—only one floor. When the doors open, the office will be on your left."

The guard turned away. Small was a little surprised. Usually, security guys liked to yak it up with ex-cops. Oh, well. They weren't paying him to be anybody's friend. He walked quickly down to the elevators and pressed the "up" button. The doors opened as if the elevator were waiting for him. He stepped inside. There were push buttons for two dozen floors, though the circles at the very top and in the subbasement had slots requiring special keys— restricted areas, no doubt. He had to go up one floor, and only one. He pressed the button for two.

The elevator was completely silent. He barely felt it move between the time the doors closed and opened again mere seconds later. He stepped out of the car and turned left.

The glass door before him had a sign that read, LILAH MORGAN: SPECIAL OPERATIONS.

This was the woman he wanted to see. From the information he could gather, she was pretty high up in the overall organization, which to Small meant only one thing: The higher up you got around here, the fatter the payday.

He pushed the door open. An attractive young woman, thin, with long dark hair, looked up from her desk. She smiled a cool, professional smile. "You must be Grady Small."

"Guilty as charged," he replied. He ran a hand over his receding hairline, still chopped short in the buzz cut he'd had since his two years in the marines. This woman was so cool, she made him a little nervous. "I'm looking for Lilah—"

"You've found her." This was the powerful Lilah Morgan? Small had expected someone older. It usually took years to claw your way up through a law firm. This must be one formidable woman. She extended her hand. Small met it with his own, much larger, fingers. They shook once. Her grip was very strong. "Won't you have a seat?"

He nodded, and managed to cram his bulk into one of the designer chairs.

Lilah remained standing. "We've got a rather unusual project here. Well, actually, everything that goes through this department is rather unusual. If you work out well on this particular assignment, we'll have other tasks for you."

That's the sort of thing Small liked to hear. Long-term employment.

"First, though, I have to ask you a few questions," the attorney continued. "Do you believe in vampires?"

"I believe in anything that lets me get a paycheck. Twenty years on the force, you see just about everything."

"Yes, I wouldn't be surprised if you had seen a thing or two that can't be explained. Well, working with us you'll see a lot more of that. Tell me, do you know a Phillip Manchester?"

"You mean that washed-up private eye?" Small said before he could stop himself. He realized he shouldn't be too hard on private dicks, since he was one himself now. "I haven't seen him in a couple years. I'd be surprised if he was still in the business."

"Our sources tell us that Mr. Manchester is currently in a coma. Unfortunately, other sources tell us they've seen the 'private eye' out on the streets. We need you to look into this for us."

"Sure." Small shrugged. "Why not?"

"Well, when you look, you'll find a surprise or two. And vampires will be only one small part of it. I'm going to send you to a special orientation before we give you the case file. Oh yes, and you'll have to sign a few papers first. I'll send you down to contracts next. Now, don't be upset if you see a couple of flashes of fire. And they will be asking for a small quantity of your blood, but that's all routine."

Small swallowed. "Blood? Contracts? We've always done business before as a handshake deal."

"We're talking too much money for handshakes." She took a pen and wrote a figure on a pad before her. "This will be your initial retainer."

Grady Small looked at the pad in awe. He had never seen so many zeros in one place.

For that kind of money, he could spare a little blood.

CHAPTER FIVE

Wesley looked up from his research. The scream came from the very back of the hotel.

"Uh, guys?" Cordy said softly. "It sounds like our demon's come down the back stairs."

"Either that or the mice are getting a little large," Lorne agreed. He picked up the crossbow he had retrieved from the weapons case. "And maybe trying to sing opera."

"So what now?" Cordy asked. "Angel told us to sit tight."

Wesley nodded. "We weren't supposed to go after the demons. But it sounds like the demons are coming to us."

"Demons?" Lorne gripped the crossbow a little tighter. "You used the plural."

Cordy looked at the back, toward where they'd heard the scream. "Well, there was that other thing that looked like Phil. . . ."

"Exactly." Wesley nodded. "We don't know the precise shape or size of this threat. There may be more than one of them loose in the hotel. We need to be prepared for anything. After all, this one might not look like Fred."

Cordy picked up on the thought. "Or it could be another Fred. Or another Phil. Or another one of any of us."

Wesley didn't think the demons had gotten close enough to copy that many of them yet. But this speculation was getting them nowhere. He needed something to keep some distance between him and the demon. He grabbed an ax from the cabinet. "I'll go take a look."

Lorne headed for the stairs. "I'll check on Angel, tell him what's happening down below."

Cordy frowned at both of them. "And I guess I'll wait patiently by the phone. If this is what I used to do, it's no wonder I lost my memory."

"Grab something from the weapons case," Wesley called over his shoulder as he headed toward the noise. "We all have to be ready to defend ourselves."

Cordy pulled a short sword from below the counter. "Hey, I haven't forgotten everything."

Wesley nodded once and headed toward the hall behind the office. He heard someone running. He hurried to follow, but not too fast. If there were more than one of them, this could be a trap.

• • •

No place was safe anymore. Every day now was a battle. Or so it seemed. Ever since Lorne had lost his beloved bar Caritas and temporarily moved in with Angel and crew, things had gone from not so good to *really* not so good.

Not that, as a demon, he had a lot of housing options, even in a place as diverse as LA. But this particular location was becoming threat central. He had grown fond of Angel and his associates. After all, they had saved Lorne's life a time or two, and he liked to think his time with them had made a contribution for the greater good—but it had been so much easier when he'd been just a simple barkeep.

He held the crossbow close as he stepped onto the second floor. It was awfully quiet up there. "Angel? Gunn? I think—"

Some inner demon sense told him to duck.

"Whoa, big boy!" Lorne shouted.

Gunn took a step back, awkwardly trying to balance the double-bladed ax he had been ready to send in Lorne's direction.

"Sorry. I was expecting a demon. Well, a different demon."

Lorne shook his head, relieved that it was still attached. "I think we're all expecting those demons, all the time. You heard that scream?"

Gunn nodded.

"We're pretty sure it came from someplace downstairs," Lorne explained. "Wesley's gone to check it out."

Gunn frowned. "By himself?"

Lorne shrugged. "Yeah, the teamwork thing doesn't seem to be working on all cylinders here."

Gunn waved his weapon down the hall. "Angel's circling around the back. We were going to meet down by the front desk. What say we give Wesley a hand?"

"That sounds like a plan."

Lorne followed Gunn down the staircase.

Cordy looked up as they reached the first floor.

"Fred called on her cell phone. I think she's on her way back. No sign of the—other Fred."

Gunn looked pained. "Fred's coming back? Didn't Angel say it was better if she stayed at the hospital?"

"Well, I tried to tell her . . . ," Cordy began with a shrug. "Fred doesn't always listen."

"Yeah," Gunn agreed. "Like I need somebody to tell me."

They were getting sidetracked again. It was time for Lorne the Social Director to get the troops back in action.

"Well, boys and girls, we'd better find the other one before the original walks through the door." Lorne waved for Gunn to follow him. He called to Cordy, "Tell Angel what's happening."

"What's happening—where?"

Angel walked into the lobby from the office. He must have come in from the back stairs, circling through the back of the hotel as Gunn had mentioned. Which meant he hadn't seen either Wesley, or the demon, on his travels.

Lorne cut to the chase. "Wes followed that noise we all heard before."

Angel scowled. "He never was any good at following orders."

"But if you didn't run into him—" Gunn began.

"It means they're downstairs." Angel nodded to Gunn. "Lorne, you should stay here. I want a couple of folks in the lobby in case anybody else decides to show up."

"Whatever you say, boss."

"Gunn?"

"I'm on it. This sucker's not getting away from me."

Lorne watched as the two walked through the doorway to the steps leading down to the basement. He exhaled heavily and collapsed in one of the lobby's overstuffed chairs. "So much for getting in on the action."

Actually, he was just as happy being on backup rather than the front lines. He was more an "entertainment demon" than an "action demon," after all.

"If you're going to get comfortable," Cordy instructed, "why not do it on the couch over there."

She pointed to the far side of the room. "That way you can watch the back entrance while I cover the front."

Lorne grabbed his crossbow and moved to the vantage point Cordy had suggested.

"I see what you mean," he said as he sat again. "With this double thing going on, I don't think any of us are going to get too comfortable for quite some time."

Wesley followed the noise, through the back hall and then down the stairs that led to Angel's training room in the basement. Wesley felt like he was being led very far away from the others. He paused halfway down the steps. Maybe he should wait, let the others know where he was going.

He heard footsteps again, still some distance away. The demon was going deeper into the basement, and was making no attempt to be quiet about it. Perhaps it wanted to escape through the tunnels below the hotel—or perhaps open those tunnels to others of its kind. If the demon held Fred's memories, it would know exactly how to get into those tunnels. If the demon doubles held some of the same memories as the original members of the team, they had no secrets whatsoever.

This was all the more reason to stop the thing now, while he still had a chance. Cordy and Lorne knew what he was doing. The others would realize he was down here any minute now. Maybe he could at least corner the demon until then.

Wesley walked quickly through Angel's room, a simple, though well-appointed space where their vampire boss could sleep without fear of sunlight. The demon was nowhere to be seen. It must have passed through the far door. The basement ran the entire length of the hotel.

Wesley heard a faint crash as he reached the second door. It sounded as though it came from the far end of the basement, maybe the room that held the huge furnace and water heaters. He stepped into a hallway immediately below the one he had just walked one floor above, but where that hall had subdued lighting behind ornate art deco fixtures, this bare hall was lit by only a row of sixty-watt bulbs hanging at intervals from the ceiling.

Wesley paused, hoping to hear some other noise. For an instant, he felt as though he were playing that old children's game of "hot and cold." He wanted the demon to call out, to tell Wesley he was practically freezing, or almost burning up.

He slowly eased down the corridor, alert for any movement. The door to one of the storage rooms was open. He heard a noise within. It sounded like sobbing.

He was getting warmer.

If it was the demon, it was certainly calling attention to itself. Why?

For the same reason the Phil-demon grabbed Fred, and the Fred-demon came back to join all of them. Because these things needed to touch each and every one of them. Preferably while alone, Wesley guessed. Maybe that way, the demons could simply kill the originals and take over without anybody knowing.

It certainly sounded like a trap. And here he was, walking right into it.

"Wesley?" Fred's voice called from beyond the open door.

He was warm enough to get a fever.

But he had to know. Why were the doubles here at Angel Investigations? And what would happen when all the doubles came into existence? The whole world seemed on the edge of chaos, but Wesley knew there were reasons buried deep within.

He paused at the open door. The room was a depository for long discarded furniture, couches, chairs, even a mattress or two, stacked haphazardly along either wall, with a narrow pathway in between the piles. Wesley detected a faint odor of rot and mildew. He couldn't think of a better place for an ambush.

He was burning up.

"Help me, Wesley."

"Certainly, Fred." Wesley stepped just inside the door. A part of him thought about the real

Fred. Once, a long time ago, he had thought the two of them might have a future together. But the demon would know that, too, and would use it against him.

Wesley seriously considered stepping back out in the hall. But he so wanted to see how the demons worked. If there was some way he could trap this abomination, keep it contained without allowing it to complete its business, there was so much he could learn. "I want to help you," he said. "But I can't help you if I don't know where you are. Now what seems to be the problem?"

Later, he wasn't exactly sure why he hadn't rushed into the hall and given a shout for help right then. Intellectual curiosity? Or blind stupidity? Perhaps a little of both.

The demon rushed him, tipping a pile of moldy mattresses to block his exit.

Wesley leaped away from the falling furniture, swinging his ax to keep the demon at bay. The creature hissed, its Fred mask wavering for an instant to show the stone face beneath.

"What? Are you hogging all the fun, Wes?"

It was Gunn's voice, right behind him.

"Yes, I never quite figured out how to share!" Wesley called, as he swung his ax a second time. The creature hissed and backed away. "However, under the circumstances, I'm willing to learn."

The demon continued to change, losing all

traces of its mortal likeness, becoming a short, stunted thing that looked like a pile of stones stacked in some rough approximation of the human form.

The stones leaped past Wesley, and landed right in front of Gunn.

The demon's face changed back to that of Fred.

"Charles," she said with a smile. Gunn's head was clouded by a glittering mist. His ax was twin bladed and twice the size of Wesley's. One swift strike, and the demon's head left its body.

The demon dissolved, going from solid stone to thick yellow liquid in an instant. The liquid evaporated almost as soon as it hit the concrete floor.

Both men stared in quiet dismay.

Angel stepped in the room. "The thing is gone already? Just like that?"

"That was unpleasant," Wesley acknowledged.

Gunn nodded, shaking the remaining liquid from his fingers. "I feel like I've been slimed."

"I'm afraid it's much worse than that." Wesley brushed past the other two to reach the relatively fresher air of the hall. "If you'll excuse me, I think it's of the utmost importance I return to my research."

Gunn wiped at his face with his sleeve. "That doesn't sound like good news, man."

Wesley shook his head. "The more I know about

what we are dealing with, the more I know they have to be stopped quickly."

Something in the rock demon's transformation had triggered a thought at the back of his brain—something he had read, back in his days as a Watcher. If he was correct, he had a good idea just where these things came from, and where they might want to go.

But before he even checked his books, Wesley knew one thing: Neither one of those places was a very good place to be.

CHAPTER SIX

Lilah Morgan reviewed the file on this latest opportunity. That's what Wolfram & Hart thought of all these demon incursions: they were opportunities. As they had learned time and time again, a demon out to conquer or destroy the world, when properly controlled, could be a most valuable commodity. And these were a particularly interesting set of demons, most likely one of the demon monastic orders, such as the Twelve Pariahs or the Assassins of Galt. The firm's computerized mystical database put the probability of the demons belonging to one of these groups at 83 percent, particularly high for this early in the investigation. If their research was correct, these were demons with a mission. All her firm had to do was determine how that mission could best benefit Wolfram & Hart.

Of course, when you were dealing with creatures

from other dimensions, there were other factors that had to be taken into consideration. With certain of the early texts in the database, the ancient authors might have added a bit of elaboration beyond the cold hard facts, like the HERE BE MONSTERS you might see on ancient maps of the unexplored world. That was the primary reason they often hired outside contractors. If the information on the new menace proved to be a tad inaccurate, contractors were always expendable.

But Lilah had a good feeling about the new hire they'd gotten to look into this, that big bruiser Grady Small. She flipped quickly to their psych summary on the former cop. He had an interesting mix of fear and aggression that could be very useful. He had killed, and killed often. Most of the deaths were in the line of duty, although a couple of the cases were a bit suspect. And he had looked the other way in one recent instance after a large amount of money had been deposited in a "secret" bank account—secret, of course, to those without her firm's resources. Yes, he had exhibited anger on occasion, but he had an odd streak of pragmatism that had let him survive every misstep until, of course, this latest incident had removed him from the force.

According to these notes, Wolfram & Hart had helped that little episode along too. It looked like her firm had had their eye on Lieutenant Small for a long time. With this new demonic opportunity, it had finally been the right moment to bring the former policeman into their employ.

Yes, there was a lot to like about this newcomer. Every now and then, new recruits survived their first assignments. She thought Small stood a real chance of being a survivor. In time, he could develop the skills to become one of their regular investigators. Stranger things had happened.

And Lilah found the presence of this latest demon infestation to be particularly interesting in regard to her long-term goals. All their earlier research at Wolfram & Hart had confirmed that Angel was central to what lay ahead. These demons' movements, infiltrating his organization, only confirmed Angel's importance in the coming apocalypse.

Wolfram & Hart liked to look at the big picture. One way or another, they would use Angel, and the demons, to their advantage. Angel was not to be touched until the time was right. That order came straight from the senior partners. But that didn't mean she couldn't encourage the demons to mess a bit with Angel's associates to see what developed.

She looked up as someone rapped sharply at her open door. It was David Marsh, her new assistant, a real eager sort. Perhaps a bit too eager.

"Yes?" she commanded, careful not to smile a

greeting. It took time to train assistants. David needed to be afraid of her. Otherwise, he'd stab her in the back in an instant. He prided himself on being on top of every development. Whenever she needed him, he seemed to be only a few feet away. Lilah thought he never left the office. He probably slept in some corner of the basement. With a personality like that, Dave was on the fast track around here. She preferred he used that track to run over someone other than Lilah Morgan.

"Sorry to disturb you," David said with an eagerness that proved he wasn't sorry at all, "but a new piece of information arrived that I thought imperative to pass on to you."

"Really?" she replied coolly.

He slipped a sheet of paper in front of her. It was the latest surveillance reports from Angel Investigations. They had brought Wesley in again. So they realized the serious nature of this as well.

Wesley. She had to concentrate to keep herself from smiling. She had to admit, a part of her wanted to protect the former Watcher. Especially since Wesley and Angel had had that falling out, and Lilah had found a way to fill a void in Wesley's life.

She also had to admit that he did something for her as well, gave her a pure physical satisfaction of the sort she would never find in the rarified atmosphere of Wolfram & Hart. It was pure animal attraction. They had a wonderful chemistry in bed together. Sometimes, though, Lilah wondered if there might be a hint of something more.

Wesley had proved useful in other ways as well. Occasionally she had been able to discretely use Wesley as a source of information. Oh, nothing too specific or damaging, just sort of the general direction Wesley might be going with Angel's detective agency.

Maybe she could get him to drop a hint or two on their next late-night rendezvous. They hadn't seen each other in days. As far as she was concerned, they were just about due.

A woman needed to have some relaxation, didn't she?

"Ms. Morgan?" David prompted.

She looked up at him sharply. "I'm sure this memo has been forwarded to my computer. What was it that you specifically wished to bring to my attention?"

David looked the slightest bit distressed. "Angel Investigations may discover the nature of these demons before we do. Do we want to intervene?"

"Negative. At this point, we're only gathering information." She rewarded him with a tight, professional smile. "If Angel and his people discover anything, we'll find a way to ascertain that as well." She paused a beat, then added, "Will that be all?"

"Yes, Ms. Morgan. Sorry to bother you, Ms. Morgan." Then David was out the door.

Lilah thought she'd handled that well. No need to let an overzealous newcomer make things complicated. It was best, especially when dealing with demons, to keep your distance until it was the time to make a decisive move. Now that Wesley was in the mix, well, perhaps she just might have to get a bit more involved.

After all, everything was an opportunity at Wolfram & Hart.

Grady Small frowned. Something was very wrong in this place.

First off, everybody was smiling. Maybe it was just the training staff, but he found their constant upbeat attitude creepier than anything in the presentation. Not that the slide and video show was any walk in the park.

Oh yes, Mr. Small. Welcome to the firm, Mr. Small. Anything you'd like, Mr. Small? He'd asked for spring water. He had thought to ask for scotch to go with it, but was all too afraid they'd oblige. No drinking on the job around here. He wanted to keep his wits as sharp as possible while on the premises.

He always figured the angles. It would pay to get on the good side of Lilah Morgan. She was one good-looking broad: thin, well dressed, put together just right. But she was a little scary, too. She had known exactly how much money the firm had to offer for him to stick around. And he was sure she'd lose no time getting rid of him if he wasn't doing the job up to her expectations.

What had he expected from this place? He was sure there would be physical danger, and that maybe he would learn a company secret or two that he didn't dare to share. He never thought he'd have to sit through hours of so-called "Orientation."

"Vampires often don't photograph well using traditional technology," the deep male announcer's voice continued. "Therefore, we offer you this dramatic reenactment."

Small looked up at the wall of video screens that fronted the classroom. He had told himself he was going to look at this with an open mind. He had seen plenty of weird stuff as an L.A. cop, how could this get any weirder?

A teen clad in black leather, looking like he had escaped from some bad biker movie, jumped out in front of another young man, this one wearing a suit.

"Excuse me," the well-dressed man said, trying to step past the other. "I was going—"

"You're finished going places!" the leather teen sneered. He had very long incisors. "Now you're going to be my dinner!"

The video image froze, showing how the teen's

face had changed. A hard ridge of flesh protruded from his forehead. His teeth were elongated and much more prominent, while his eyes had sunken behind his bulging brows.

"The stranger has revealed himself to be a vampire," the announcer's smooth voice continued. "And how do you deal with a vampire? The most efficient method is with a wooden stake."

This was a little crazy, wasn't it? But nobody else in the room was laughing, especially not the guys who already worked for the law firm. Open mind, Small reminded himself.

The video image jumped back to live action as the man with the suit withdrew a foot-long piece of wood from some inner pocket.

"Whoa!" the vampire cried in surprise. But the man in the suit had already pushed the stake forward and down, plunging it into the vampire's chest. The vampire dissolved in a puff of smoke and falling ashes.

"The threat is ended, quickly and cleanly," the announcer continued. "Later, you will all have a chance to practice this particular killing technique. It might save your lives."

So they were going to practice killing? Small supposed it would be better than sitting here stuffed in this chair.

"Now, what if you are confronted by a group of vampires? Or if you have to deal with some different creature of the night? The security team at Wolfram and Hart has devised many successful techniques for the subjugation or termination of hundreds of different threats to your safety."

The scene shifted. Three men in suits were confronted by three others. One was the vampire from the last scene. The other two were all green and lumpy, like they'd stepped out of a grade-Z monster movie.

"Remember, when confronted by the unknown, keep an open mind. Don't make assumptions. Our information archives are the best in the world, and we will do our best to keep you informed of every possibility you may encounter."

The men in suits each pulled out slim handguns of a sort unknown to Small. They quickly shot the three they faced. The guns made no noise. The camera showed a close-up of a dart sticking from the vampire's neck.

"Whenever possible," the announcer continued, "if you are working on an active case, we prefer capture to killing. Remember, it is much harder, though not impossible, to get information from the recently deceased."

On screen, another pair of vampires jumped out from behind a Dumpster to confront the men in suits. One of the well-dressed fellows hit the first vampire with a kick to the stomach; another guy flipped the second vampire over his shoulder. It reminded Small of some demented kung fu movie.

"Make sure you are properly prepared for the field," the announcer droned on. "We will make every attempt to keep you informed of any danger. Your safety is our primary concern."

"Your safety is our primary concern?" It was the same sort of bull they used to feed him on the force.

Some of the other guys in the orientation room shifted in their seats. A couple of them coughed nervously. He was surrounded by a bunch of wusses.

Small knew his way around a fight. He was sure that was one reason they'd hired him. If he was going to come up against some new kind of bad guy, he was sure he'd be able to fight them, too. With all this money they were paying him, he expected to have to handle something new.

"Now," the announcer's voice droned on, "let's familiarize ourselves with some of the mystical weapons you might encounter."

Well, maybe not this new. First vampires, and now magic? Small sighed. With what they were showing him now, he imagined he was in this for good. Retirement from Wolfram & Hart probably involved a pine box.

This was only the beginning, Small reminded himself. It had to get better from here. With this money, he could buy a better class of doughnut. Now he just had to live long enough to enjoy it.

CHAPTER SEVEN

Gunn cleaned himself up, changed his clothes, and headed back down to the lobby. He still felt dirty. He thought that, once he had a chance to talk to Fred, maybe they'd move their stuff to a different room—one that hadn't been visited by a demon.

He looked below as he headed down the stairs.

Fred was giving Wesley a hand with the books, splitting up the research, while Cordy studied a computer screen. Angel stood in the corner, drinking a tall glass of pig's blood.

No one was saying a word.

Gunn spun around as he heard a noise above him. It was Lorne, following him down the stairs. Gunn could hear his own heart pounding in his ears. He guessed he was a little jumpy.

Lorne looked past him to the crowd below. "Not exactly a party atmosphere."

Gunn shook his head. "I guess we've got to wait for our demon doubles before we really cut loose."

Angel put down his empty glass and stepped forward as Gunn and Lorne reached the bottom of the stairs. "It's time to change the rules here, people." He nodded to Fred. "Seeing somebody who looks just like you or somebody you know would freak out anybody. But so far, we've just been reacting."

"And they're probably out there making more of us," Cordy added.

Gunn agreed all too much with that. "So what have we done, except given them more of what they want?"

"Well, we have seen them up close," Wesley said. "That should help with my research."

Gunn had seen them up close twice. It hadn't gotten any prettier the second time. "And what has your research done for us so far?"

"Observing their behavior helps me narrow things down to certain demon subspecies." Wesley closed the book in front of him. "I believe their real purpose is to infect us all."

Gunn thought again of the slime on his skin. "What, then? Do they kill us? Replace us?"

"Seems to make as much sense as anything," Angel agreed. "But we don't know why they're doing this."

Wesley nodded. "Some of us—maybe only one

in particular—must be important to their rituals."

"We're all tied up in this somehow, then," Lorne said.

"*All* of us?" Cordy asked with a frown.

Angel looked up. "Are they going to go after Connor?"

Angel's son had set himself up in a loft a few blocks away while he sorted through his feelings.

Cordy's frown deepened. "Maybe one of us should check on him."

"Normally, I'd say he could take care of himself," Wesley replied. "But this is out of everybody's league."

Gunn wanted to make sure he had this whole thing right. "So what you're saying is, these demons don't care as long as they reach somebody new with their slime."

What was that? Gunn heard a long bang at the back of the hotel.

"Back door," Angel announced suddenly. He ran toward the noise.

Gunn and Wesley were right behind him.

The door had been kicked in with considerable force. Part of the frame had splintered off with it. It opened into a medium-sized room that had probably been connected to some sort of receiving dock when this place actually was a hotel.

Gunn had to admire the force behind that kind of blow. He could probably pull it off, and of course so could Angel, but he thought it was beyond anybody else here.

"Hey, there!" a voice called from behind a pile of boxes. "I just wanna talk!"

Wesley waved for Gunn to back up out of sight, then turned and called, "Gunn? Is that you?"

"Who do ya think it is?" came the angry reply.

Gunn realized he was listening to himself—well, a version of himself. The creature who spoke sounded like an earlier version of himself, when he used to run with a gang of vampire hunters and thought it was cool to mumble. This demon was copying Gunn's earlier, angrier self.

"What do you demons want?" Angel asked.

"Hey, I don't care what the other guys want!" the angry Gunn replied. "I'm out for myself here! And I'm thinking we might cut ourselves a deal!"

Angel took a step toward the voice. "A deal? What kind of a deal?"

The other Gunn leaped out of hiding. "A deal where you all die!"

The demon was surrounded once more by that odd, sparkling mist. But he was all alone. Angel had leaped out of the way the instant the creature had appeared, while Wesley and Gunn still waited by the far door.

The mist evaporated. The fake Gunn swore, and ran through the open door.

"Oh, hell," Gunn whispered. Now he would have to kill himself.

"Is he gone?" Wesley asked.

Angel moved cautiously toward the back door. "I think we need to find out."

"We may have neutralized him for now," Wesley pointed out. "It may take time to regenerate that mist."

Who were they kidding? "I think we've got to do a lot more than neutralize that sucker," Gunn said.

"What happened?" Cordy and Lorne had shown up behind Wesley.

"We've got another Gunn," Wesley explained, "but he ran out the door."

"He got away?" Cordy asked.

"No, he didn't."

Angel disappeared out the door.

Angel would put an end to this.

He picked up the creature's trail fifty feet from the door of the hotel.

The demon walked across town. He just walked, at a quick and steady pace, as if he knew just where he was going. No demon tricks, either—no flying, no disappearing from one place and popping up someplace else, no grabbing a taxi or even taking the bus. Just walking.

It felt as though the creature knew it would take over the world, but wasn't in all that much of a hurry to get it done. The Gunn-thing proceeded with a fast, deliberate stride. It detoured once around an intersection that held a couple of police cars, and retreated into the shadows when confronted by large groups of people. But mostly it just walked.

Whatever it was, it wasn't used to being followed by a vampire. It never looked back, only moved in pretty much a straight line toward its destination. Angel watched mostly from the shadows, moving casually when he might be seen by his prey, more quickly when the demon was blocked from view.

Six blocks from the hotel, Angel realized that somebody was following him, too—he heard a pattern of footsteps behind him, heavy steps made with leather-soled shoes, close but never too close, plus the faint but distinct smell of the living when the wind was right. He would have realized he had company sooner if he hadn't been concentrating on the creature in front of him.

The man following him smelled human, a mixture of sweat and stale cigarette smoke. But the demon that Angel trailed didn't smell that much different. Angel considered his options. He could take the third party out, but he risked losing the thing he followed, or worse, alerting the demon to his presence.

But chances were good the third party couldn't move like a vampire.

Angel quickly turned a corner, putting a building between himself and his pursuer, and looked for the easiest way to the roof. He spotted a fire escape, the kind with a retractable ladder to keep it out of the reach of burglars, maybe ten feet above the ground. It was an easy leap for one of his kind. He caught the black metal bars at the bottom of the rig, and swung himself onto the metal stairway. He was up on the roof before his pursuer could round the corner.

He crossed the roof quickly to see Gunn's double maybe half a block ahead. They were on a broad avenue full of one- and two-story standalone stores and small strip malls. The roofs were built close enough that Angel could easily jump between them, only having to descend to the street when they crossed the occasional boulevard. They moved more than another dozen blocks in this way.

The demon walked without stopping, twenty blocks, then thirty—Angel would have lost count if he'd had anything else to do but follow. He tried to see if there was anything unusual about the creature he followed, but it looked and moved just like Charles Gunn, a guy who didn't call attention to himself but could handle anything that came to him on the street. It made Angel think about what he and his crew had built together, back at the Hyperion Hotel.

Mostly, he thought about what he could lose.

When he had come to Los Angeles four years ago, he had already made a conscious decision to change his ways. Working with the Slayer, Buffy Summers, and her crew back in Sunnydale had convinced him he could still have a purpose, but he'd needed to leave Buffy and the others behind in order to forge his own destiny.

He had chosen to help people so he could right some small part of the wrong he had done, back when he was Angelus, before the gypsies had cursed him with his soul. What better destiny than to become a detective, dealing with cases on the supernatural underside of L.A., a part of the city where even the authorities were afraid to look?

But it had become more than that as the months had turned to years. A half-man, half-demon named Doyle had gotten Angel to look at his place in all of this at first, but then Doyle had gotten killed by the forces of darkness. By then, Cordelia had joined him, soon followed by Wesley—two from his Sunnydale days. He had gained other allies since—Gunn, Lorne, and Fred. And now his son, Connor, had dropped into the mix—a young man with amazing abilities and an enduring distrust of his father. Each of them brought their own strengths to the team. Despite their difficulties, Angel knew he would be lost without them.

Now, most of all, he wanted to protect his friends. While he had found a sort of redemption with Buffy Summers and her gang, this was the first time he'd truly felt he had the possibility of a home, a place he could truly call his own. And he wouldn't let anyone, whether it was Wolfram & Hart or a gang of body-snatching demons, take that away from him.

He came to the end of the rooftops. A large vacant lot stretched before him. The neighborhood was changing again. They had left the commercial district that bordered the old hotel, and were in a corner of the city near the freeways that held row after row of warehouses, low-slung, brick buildings that looked more or less alike save for the signs above the doors:

INTERNATIONAL FRUIT
INTERSTATE MEAT
WESTERN DRY GOODS

Angel jumped from the roof, landing softly in the dirt and weeds of the lot. The Gunn-thing, maybe a hundred yards ahead, kept on walking.

Angel couldn't think of a better place than this neighborhood for a demonic hideout. There were never that many people out on foot in most parts of L.A. Around here, there were none.

Angel looked back up the street in the direction they had come, but there was no one else to be seen. Whoever had been following him was long gone. Maybe, after he had handled the demons, he would look into who was so interested in the movements of Angel Investigations.

He jogged out of the lot and into the street, slowing to a walk. He didn't even know if he should try to look natural. Should the Gunn thing turn around, he would know he was being followed—the streets were empty: no people, no cars, just one demon and one vampire. These square, featureless buildings didn't afford much in the way of a hiding place. Angel still kept as close to the buildings as possible. Gunn Two might not see him yet, but the demons might have some sort of guard or lookout. Angel wanted to keep an element of surprise for as long as possible.

The double continued walking for a couple more blocks, finally stepping into one of the nearly identical buildings. The name over its door was DEEVER INSTRUMENTS.

What now? He had a cell phone in the pocket of his leather jacket. Not that he could get the thing to work properly. Angel was never very good with technology.

The demon had probably led Angel straight to its lair. He should probably take a closer look, make sure the thing hadn't discovered it was being followed, and had just gone into that place to shake the tail. Once he'd gotten a better idea of what was going on, the layout and all, he could go back and get the others. Besides, while these creatures could change shape, they didn't seem to have any other powers. If he got into any difficulty, he should be able to handle himself, one on one. After the way the demons had been messing up their lives, a little counter-demon action sounded good.

So now Angel had a plan. He would gather a little more information, and maybe kick some demon butt.

What could go wrong with that?

Eight hours of intensive training, and now this? Grady Small sucked on his Marlboro. He swore he was going to quit, any day now. He wanted to be around to spend all the loot this new job would get him.

He was going to quit, and soon—someday when he didn't have to stand around and watch.

Lilah Morgan's assistant, David, had been waiting for Small when he came out of the training room, and handed him his first assignment. Surveillance, of a hotel that held a crew called Angel Investigations. Small knew them a little from his days on the force. They were a strange and quiet bunch that, unlike a lot of private dicks, liked to fly under the radar and not get involved with the cops—which, as long as they didn't do anything illegal, was fine with most of the cops as well.

But there was a new wrinkle here. This same

Angel had gotten mentioned in the training. They had said he was a vampire, a very special vampire, off-limits, not to be touched. It was one of many facts in the training that got dropped on them without much explanation.

Still, surveillance? It seemed like something of a comedown after getting hired by some big guns like Wolfram & Hart, but Small guessed that investigative work was still pretty much the same, no matter how much you were being paid.

David had explained it to Small, smiling like all the others. His training would continue every day. Until Small knew enough about the new risks of the job, it was best he handled something familiar.

Part of Small wanted to push those smiles down all their throats. But then he thought again of all those zeroes. Damn it, Grady. What money can make you do.

So, surveillance it was.

He cased the hotel when he first arrived, and decided that sitting in his car would be too conspicuous. The street in front of the hotel—a bus stop book-ended between a pair of fire hydrants—was a no parking zone. He parked his car around the corner, close enough so he could get to it if he needed. Then he stood in the shadows of a tree on the far side of the street, the only light the tip of his glowing cigarette.

Nothing happened for the first hour or so. Then a young black male—the firm's information packet identified him as Charles Gunn—walked up to the hotel but didn't go inside. He was looking for something on the outside of the hotel. Small wished he could get a little closer for a better look, but didn't want to blow his cover. He strolled casually down his side of the street to keep Gunn in sight.

Gunn moved around a building to a rear door, tried the knob, but could not enter. The door must be locked. Gunn stood there for one long moment, took a deep breath, and kicked the door open. He went inside.

Within seconds, Small heard raised voices. A moment later, Gunn was out the busted door at a dead run.

He slowed down half a block away. Nobody appeared to be following him. Gunn started to walk back.

Nobody seemed to have followed him out. Wait a second. Small caught a glimpse of a guy in a black leather jacket, hanging back in the shadows.

This would be Angel.

So . . . did his crew have some sort of falling out? There was some kind of story here. Small would hang back a little bit and follow both of them for a bit.

The Wolfram & Hart–issue cell phone felt heavy

in his raincoat pocket. He wondered if he should call in this change of plan.

The training had told him that vampires had very sensitive hearing. He probably didn't want to do any talking for now.

He wondered if he should get the LaSabre. Nah. The car would be too conspicuous. It was time for some shoe leather.

He was only supposed to observe, after all.

He kept well back. He'd been at this too long to make some rookie mistake. But he kept the lean man in the black leather jacket in sight for maybe eight blocks, until he turned a corner, and the street was empty.

Angel was gone.

Not right, not left. No closing doors, no passing cars on the street. One minute the vampire was right in front of him, the next he was nowhere.

He thought again about some of the things the training session had told him about vampires. About the way they could leap and climb the sides of buildings. He had been relieved to hear that the whole bat thing had been an old wives' tale. But still, Angel could be anywhere—above him, below in the sewers.

Maybe Angel figured he was being followed. Angel could be stalking Grady now.

Maybe, Small thought, he'd better go back to the hotel.

But that was the training talking. All that mystical bull gave him the creeps. Small was on to something here.

They had been walking in a straight line across town. He'd walk another half a dozen blocks and see if he could pick up the trail.

He supposed he should have called this in, but he wasn't used to relying on other people. He'd have to find somebody he could trust in Wolfram & Hart, somebody he could really talk to. That shouldn't be so hard—after all, they were all looking for the same thing.

"I wouldn't be sticking my nose where it didn't belong."

The voice came from behind him. Small spun around, his hand already on the handle of the gun in his shoulder holster. "What are you doing here?" Small demanded.

It was Phil Manchester.

He was doubly surprised to see old Phil. The two had had a few run-ins while Grady Small had still been on the force. They had never been pleasant. Some PIs understood what it took to work with a man like Small. Phil wasn't one of them.

That wasn't the surprising part, though. According to Small's briefing, Phil was still in the hospital. "I thought you were in a coma or somethin'," Small volunteered.

Phil smiled at that. "I don't have time to sleep

when there's scum like you on the street."

That didn't sound like Phil Manchester. The skinny git had always kept his anger under wraps.

"But that's all going to change, Grady," Manchester continued. "I was thinking maybe we should get a little better acquainted."

What the hell did that mean? Small pulled out his piece. "Keep your distance!"

"Ah Grady, Grady." Before today, Manchester had never called him by his first name—ever. "I'm about to become your best friend."

This was sounding like a threat. Manchester obviously didn't know what he was getting into.

"It's you who doesn't know squat!" Small waved his gun dismissively. "I've got powerful friends these days!"

"The very reason why we picked you."

We? Small thought. *Who was we?*

Manchester kept walking toward him. "You're not working for the cops anymore, are you?"

Was it that obvious?

"So you're private, just like me. With your connections, you're probably working for somebody big-time."

"Bigger than you, punk."

Manchester shook his head. "I wouldn't have that attitude. Things are changing around here. Whether you like it or not, from here on in, Grady boy, we're working together." Manchester was smiling from ear to ear. His grin looked like death.

This was crazy. "What's up with you, Phil?"

"My mistake. I'll be working with another Grady Small. But that won't matter, 'cause you'll be dead." Phil reached in his pocket and pulled out a .38.

This was doubly crazy. How did Manchester think he was going to get away with this?

"Thank you for your life," Phil said. "Such a pitiful little thing for such a great cause."

Well, when faced by crazy, Small got crazy too. He rushed forward, grabbing Manchester's gun hand. He pushed his own piece forward and shot blind three times. He thought Manchester took all three of them in the chest.

Phil stepped away. He was still smiling. "Oh Grady, I hope that made you feel better. We'll be seeing you shortly."

And with that, the guy he thought was Phil just seemed to fall apart. Grady Small was surrounded by some sort of mist, and Phil had changed from a human being to a bunch of thick yellow liquid without a container. The slime splashed to the ground and got all over Small.

This had gone beyond crazy. This guy wasn't even human.

The thing had melted into a puddle of muck before him.

At least he thought the stuff was muck. Within

seconds, the street was dry again. But his clothes still felt soaked.

Well, in that never-ending orientation they had told him they could clean just about anything. If he had to get involved with freaks, at least they were high-tech freaks.

Maybe he'd better check in with Wolfram & Hart, just in case.

CHAPTER EIGHT

Angel approached the building cautiously, looking for any movement. The windows were dark, and the nearest streetlight had been broken. The street was quieter than a couple of tombs Angel had known, with only the occasional, distant scuffling noise of some small animal burrowing in the trash.

As he got closer, Angel realized that Deever Instruments had seen better days. Some of the windows were broken, and the front door hung a little off its frame. The place had probably been empty long before any demons moved in.

Angel pulled the door open. It might have been broken, but it made no noise. The front hallway was a mess, strewn with papers, broken furniture, even some empty fast-food sacks. Perhaps this place had been home to squatters. Angel wondered what the demons might have done with them.

He moved slowly into the unlit building, ducking a cobweb, stepping carefully over a moldy pile of files. Apparently the current occupants weren't too keen on housekeeping, either. He skirted a hole in the linoleum. Something had eaten straight through the floor, down to the dirt and concrete of the foundation. He hoped it wasn't the guys he was after.

As he slowly made his way through the debris, he heard the faint sounds of voices. He reached a cross-corridor. The voices were coming from the left, clearer now than before. This inner corridor was relatively trash free, with just an overturned wastebasket and a few discarded candy wrappers. He crept toward a double door. He could make out some of the words.

"Another. Another."

"Two more. Two."

"We are ever nearer. Ever nearer."

The words sounded like a chant. Demons were always messing with this mystical stuff. It came with the territory.

Well, he hated to break up a party, but he was going to find out just why these guys were here. He pushed on the right side of the double door. It made a soft *whooshing* sound as it opened into what Angel guessed was once a large storeroom.

A group huddled together in the huge room's midpoint, maybe fifty yards away. All were looking at the floor. None of them noticed he had entered. It took a moment to see how many were actually in front of him. They shifted slightly as they spoke, heads bobbing up and down as they chanted the same sort of words that he had heard outside. He counted seven heads in all. The way they huddled close, almost on top of one another, they looked more like one creature than seven demonic doubles.

Angel walked toward the center of the room, making no attempt to hide himself. He wanted to catch their reaction. If the going got rough, hey, that's when it was convenient to be a vampire.

Were any of them ever going to turn around? Still, they chanted and bobbed those heads. Whatever was happening, it took all their attention.

Angel stopped about twenty feet away. "Hey, guys!" he called. "Is that any way to treat a guest?"

Six heads all turned to look at him.

They had reverted to their shorter, stockier, rock demon shapes—all but one, whose human guise seemed to shimmer as Angel watched. At first, he thought he was looking at an attractive, well-built woman pushing forty—the sort of ageless, impeccably dressed woman you saw around L.A. all the time. A flash of bright green light, and the woman seemed to have no shape at all, just a random collection of hair and clothes and skin and eyes, all swimming in a liquid pool of radiance.

"Ewwwww," Angel said softly. "Not the sort of change that I would like to see."

All the rock creatures were quickly taking human form.

A thin, older man stared in fury at Angel. "What is *he* doing here?"

Gunn's double stepped forward with a grin. "He followed me. I figured it would be easier to take him out as a group."

So this not-Gunn knew he'd been following him? So much for vampire stealth.

"Who gave you the authority to make that decision?" the older one demanded.

The Gunn-demon laughed. "Certainly not you, fool. I'm used to makin' my own decisions."

"You've come to join us, Angel?" The thing that looked like Fred smiled coquettishly. "I knew you couldn't stay away."

"Yeah, it's great that you're makin' it easy for us," the Gunn-creature joined in with a grin. "I mean, not that I couldn't take out a punk vampire anytime I wanted to."

He grabbed a length of pipe from the warehouse floor. These guys might have been demons, but when in human form, they acted like flesh-and-blood mortals. That, Angel figured, gave the advantage to the vampire.

"A pipe?" Angel made a *tsking* sound. "You may look like Gunn, but you don't play fair."

The demon stepped forward, twirling the pipe like a baton. "What's the matter? The big bad vampire can't take on the little guy from the street?"

"Oh, please," Angel replied.

Angel made a quick move to knock the pipe from the fake Gunn's hand.

The demon turned in an instant, blocking the vampire's kick with its shoulder and arm. The pipe in the demon's other hand connected with Angel's ankle.

Pain shot up Angel's leg. That kind of move might have broken some bones in a human. But that wasn't what worried Angel.

The demon had guessed what Angel was going to do. He had fought side by side with Charles Gunn for more than three years. Gunn knew all his moves. That meant the demon knew his moves as well.

So much, then, for the element of surprise.

Maybe the vampire didn't have quite as much of an advantage as he had thought.

Angel retreated, putting a few paces between himself and his all-too-knowledgeable opponent.

"Are you coming to me for help, Angel?" The Fred demon smiled coquettishly. "You know you've always wanted me."

No, he hadn't. Winifred Burkle was an attractive woman and all, but frankly, ever since he rescued her from that demon dimension, he'd felt more protective of her than anything else. Early on, he thought Fred had a bit of a crush on him. He'd thought it was kind of sweet. But that was it. Not to mention the whole fall-in-love-with-a human/lose-your-soul part of the gypsy curse that put him off dating most humans anyway.

Fred took a step toward him. "I don't have the hang-ups of my twin. I think it would be fun with a vampire."

She was trying to distract him. He spun around. Two human-demons he didn't recognize were creeping up behind him. They stopped as he feinted toward them. But Angel didn't want to commit himself to any single opponent. The demons meant to confuse him, then overwhelm him with their numbers.

This was crazy. They not only knew his moves, they knew his mind.

Maybe Angel had been a little too confident, waltzing into the demons' lair. He could handle six of anything in the real world. But this wasn't the real world, and some of these guys knew him all too well.

Well, Angel thought, *this was an information-gathering assignment, after all*—and he'd certainly gotten some information.

The demons all stopped and groaned as one. They turned to look back from where they had come.

The light pulsed behind them once more. Another figure was forming in the glow. He was a tall, heavyset guy, wearing a worn raincoat over a wrinkled suit. Maybe the original version had been a cop.

Demon butt-kicking was looking more difficult with every passing moment. Maybe Angel should just concentrate on getting out alive so all this information could be of some use.

The Gunn-double looked at Angel and grinned. "Looks like I got me a vamp to kill."

"What are you doing?" the older demon insisted. "I'm the eldest. I give the orders."

The heavyset guy in the raincoat stepped away from the others.

"I can handle myself," the demon announced. "I'll take him out in a second."

Well, now. This was the sort of macho bull that Angel could deal with. He let the heavyset demon rush him, then spun and kicked the creature right in the solar plexus.

The kick lifted the demon up into the air. He crashed into a pile of steel drums, a crumpled heap that dissolved a few seconds later into the same yellow slime.

The remaining demons hesitated for an instant.

"Made you think twice, huh?" Angel called out.

But all six remaining creatures had turned to look at the spot they had all been clustered around when Angel first entered the room. They groaned softly.

For the first time, Angel saw a small crystal, pulsing with a bright green light where it lay upon the floor. The light seemed to produce more of that yellow slime, but instead of disappearing, the slime joined together, the green glow increasing all around it as the slime coalesced into human form.

In a matter of seconds, the heavyset fellow was back in their midst.

The demon flexed its recently re-formed arms and shoulders. "You got me with a lucky punch. Care to try again?"

So this was what happened to the demons when Angel and company thought they had died. They would regenerate themselves. He could kill them over and over again, and they wouldn't stay dead.

The Gunn thing stepped in front of him. "Enough of your muscling in. I think we should keep this fight in the family."

The Gunn-demon lunged for Angel's legs.

Angel kicked him out of the way, dancing away from the semicircle. Whatever happened, he wanted to keep away from the slime.

Angel waved to the remaining demons. "Maybe I'll be going."

All seven of them rushed him with a roar. But Angel had already backpedaled out the storeroom door, and used his night vision to navigate his way through the trash-strewn hallway in a matter of seconds. He ran across the still empty street, heading for the relative safety of the rooftops that had brought him here.

Maybe not his coolest exit, Angel thought. But he was in one piece, he hadn't been slimed, and he had some information that would greatly help identify and defeat these things.

It was a first step, nothing more. But it finally gave Angel and his crew a chance to get to the demons, before the demons got to all of them.

There was more than one way to kick demon butt, after all.

CHAPTER NINE

Lorne looked out over the assembled troops, once again gathered in the lobby of the Hyperion Hotel. They were all working, but they didn't feel right. And it wasn't just that Angel was missing, out there somewhere, chasing demons by himself. It was that the we're-all-in-this-together banter was just plain gone from this place, replaced by a quiet that was downright creepy.

Not only did they need to figure out exactly what they were facing—but when and why they were facing them too. Until they determined what the rules were for these particular demons—and demons always had rules; they had so many rules on Lorne's homeworld, he had up and left—they had to be aware of just about everything.

Take Fred, for instance. She had insisted on coming back from the hospital. Something about Phil being in a coma, surrounded by police, and she needed to get some sleep. But was it the real Fred who had walked through the door? Was it even the real Fred who had insisted on coming back?

She certainly seemed nice enough to be the actual Fred. She had waved and smiled and chatted with all of them, then had run clear across the room to give Gunn a hug. None of that diva-on-a-bad-day attitude of the last Fred who had graced their presence. From what Lorne had seen with Fred and heard about the fake Phil, there seemed to be an edge to the demons that wasn't present in the real deal. He wondered if the doubles were always angry, always ready to take offense, sort of like the real deals on their worst days. There had to be something in this that they could use. If, of course, Lorne wasn't missing something else.

Would they have to wonder every time anybody walked through the door? This was a job for Krevlornswath of the Deathwok Clan. Well, maybe it was more of a job for the guy who used to run Caritas.

"Okay, children!" he called to the assembled masses. "I believe it's time for a new tradition!"

"Which is?" Cordy asked in her best I-used-to-be-a-cheerleader upbeat way. Lorne realized that even those who weren't empathic demons might be feeling the negative vibes.

Lorne squared his shoulders, shook his arms, and gave the room his best show-business grin. "I like to call it the 'Every Time Somebody Walks Through the Door Sing-a-thon'! Sort of a 'We Are the World' for the Hyperion Hotel. A campfire sing-along type thing. Except without the campfire."

Wesley looked up from his reading. "It would certainly give us a much needed feeling of safety."

"Since we can never be sure if the rest of us are really—us?" Gunn asked.

"So are we ready to show what we're really made of?" Did Lorne detect a hint of tentativeness in Fred's voice?

"Why wouldn't we be?" Cordelia demanded. "I mean—is this really necessary? I've barely moved away from this desk."

"Often managing the whole of Angel Investigations all by yourself," Lorne replied with a smile. "That's the very attitude that, under these circumstances, demands a song." He paused, once more surveying the room with his 100-watt smile. "So everybody ready?"

"I'll go first," Fred volunteered. "Well, I'm the most likely—you know."

Lorne nodded. Indeed she was.

"Just sing something you're comfortable with," he suggested. "Then we can go right around the room."

Fred sang the chorus of an Irish drinking song.

Wesley sang a bit of a Beatles tune.

Gunn sang a few bars of "My Girl."

Cordy sighed and said, "Well, if everybody's doing it." She sang some of that song from *Cats*. Memories, indeed.

They all turned to Lorne. Oh, my.

Gunn broke the silence that followed. "We all okay?"

Lorne thought about it for a moment. His readings were the slightest bit off, he thought, for two different reasons.

"It always helps when people sing, don't you think? Just lightens the mood, beefs up the energy—well . . ." Lorne realized he was stalling. "I did notice a new bit or two."

He looked at each of the women. Cordy and Fred both frowned back. He nodded to Gunn. Gunn did not look pleased.

"Now with Cordy," Lorne continued, "I'm thinking she might still have a little bit of that higher power thing going on. Plus, of course, she was part demon before all this happened. She's got a lot going on in there. But she doesn't sound at all like our demon doubles."

Cordy looked a bit perplexed. "Maybe I should have sung something from *Les Mis*?"

Lorne shook his head gently. "It shouldn't be surprising, considering all that you've been through. Maybe more is going on than simply losing your memory. Maybe your aura has to sort itself out as well."

"So I've got to jump-start my aura?" Cordy shrugged and smiled tentatively. "Sounds good—I guess."

Lorne turned to the more difficult of the pair. "It's a different thing entirely than what's inside Fred."

"Something's inside me?" Fred did not seem pleased by the prospect.

"I think it's a bit of the demon that attacked you. When they take your pattern—the blueprint of you, I guess you could call it—they appear to leave the slightest little bit behind. A marker of some sort. I sense it in Gunn, too, though in him it's not quite as strong."

Lorne shrugged. "Before you ask, I have no idea why."

"But doesn't it sound like they might be linked to us somehow?" Fred asked. "And the link might get stronger over time?"

"Like a homing device?" Gunn added, sounding no less upset. "Then there would be no way to get away from the things."

"Except probably to destroy them," Wesley chimed in. "But I think we knew that already." He looked back to the book in front of him. "This will narrow down my search considerably."

"I'm a demon-homing device?" Gunn repeated. "This is definitely not cool."

"It's probably better than whatever comes next," Fred added.

"Thanks for reminding me," Gunn replied.

Well hey, Lorne thought, *at least I've got them all talking.* Maybe he had a future as a social director on an all-demon cruise. If demons took cruises.

Wesley slapped his hand flat down on the book in front of him, raising a cloud of dust. "I think I've got it!"

"Who we're facing?" Cordy asked

"And it's even worse than you thought," Fred added.

"Well, yes," Wesley said with a grin. "But when has that ever stopped us?"

Lorne smiled. It was nice to have the old gang back.

Angel quickly reached the first of the rooftops. He bent close to the asphalt, crouching on hands and knees. Only the top of his head showed over the lip of the roof as he looked back to the building on the other side of the broad avenue. So far, there was no evidence that he was being followed.

As though on cue, the front door banged open, and three of the demonic humans strode out onto the nighttime street. They were making no attempt to be quiet.

In fact, they were arguing. It struck Angel then: Except for that moment when he'd caught them in their ritual, weren't they *always* arguing?

The heavyset guy whom Angel had tossed around inside the warehouse stepped in front of the other two. From a distance, the guy definitely acted and moved like a cop. Well, if the demons were going to make doubles, it made sense to copy people in authority.

A cab pulled around the corner, then slowed to a stop in front of the three. If they called a taxi, that meant they had other plans. Unless they were planning to use the ride to beat Angel back to the hotel.

He pulled out the cell phone Fred had stuffed in his pocket in the vain hope he might be able to use it.

"Well, Angel," he could still hear her saying, "catch up to the twenty-first century."

He started pressing buttons.

Nothing happened. A red light blinked dully.

NO CHARGE. Guess you couldn't leave these things in your pocket for weeks.

He leaned over the edge of the roof to catch the directions the demon gave to the cab driver. He recognized the street address before the demon added three final words:

"Wolfram and Hart."

Were these guys working for the lawyers? If so,

why hide out in a warehouse that had seen better days?

Well, one more thing to tell the others. He needed to get back to the hotel as quickly as possible.

CHAPTER TEN

They grabbed him before he could even walk in the front door. Men in heavy white space suits appeared as he crossed the plaza in front of Wolfram & Hart, their voices muffled behind thick faceplates.

"I'm afraid we need to detain you, Mr. Small."

"Nothing to be alarmed about, Mr. Small."

"This is merely routine, Mr. Small."

Routine? Small thought as they grabbed his arms. Routine for what? "What's going on?" he asked as they pulled him to the ground. "Did I do something?"

Six strong men in white surrounded him, blocking his view of the rest of the plaza.

"It's not what you did. It's whom you met."

They covered him with a white sheet, then bound his arms and legs. With this kind of greeting, he half-expected he'd be taken upstairs and dissected.

He was lifted by a half dozen sets of hands onto a stretcher. Two more straps were tightened over his chest and legs.

"What are you doing to me?" he shouted as they began pushing the stretcher.

"It's for your own safety, Mr. Small," one of the muffled voices replied. "Our sensors have detected a change in your aura."

"A change in my aura?" What the hell did that mean?

Wolfram & Hart talked a good game: All the money and influence you could get if you became part of their team. But Small realized he had no idea what their real agenda was. He had known, even back when he used to work with them while he was still on the force, that most of what the firm did was off the traditional—and probably legal—radar. By working so quietly, they got away with things, things they wouldn't be held responsible for in the court of public opinion. Sometimes they could simply ignore the law.

A few hours ago, Small had thought it wonderful to be recruited for such an all-powerful organization. Now he wasn't so sure.

It occurred to him, as they wheeled him to who-knew-where, that this might be a test. They had told him his training would be ongoing. What if this was only a part of that—an exercise to see how he'd react under stress? After all, they had restrained him, nothing more. Maybe he was being graded on his reactions even now. Like a pop quiz with Halloween costumes.

Or maybe he had really screwed up, and this aura thing was grounds for immediate dismissal. Except Grady Small suspected that when they terminated you at Wolfram & Hart, they really terminated you. He never thought he would personally be testing that theory quite this soon.

Basically, he wasn't quite sure if this was a death sentence or the company version of a fraternity hazing. Maybe no amount of money was worth this. He wished they'd take off the sheet.

He heard the muffled voices tell people to "Make way! Make way!" He heard no questions or surprised voices at his passing. Maybe the folks on the plaza saw men in hazard suits with gurneys and bundled bodies every day around here.

The gurney stopped. He heard doors *thunk* shut, the soft *whir* of a service elevator—the way sound echoed in here, it was the kind with shiny metal walls and no Muzak. Doors opened. He was on the move again.

"Out of the way!" someone shouted. "Code green!"

A heavy door opened with a rush of air, as if they were passing into a sealed vault.

Small heard a great deal of rhythmic, organized movement around him as he felt the pressure ease up on his chest and legs. They were removing the straps.

"Clear the room!"

A heavy metal door shut with a loud *clang*.

The sheet was pulled off Small's head. He was staring at a white ceiling. The lighting was quite bright, but indirect. He couldn't determine the source. He turned his head. A number of small, sophisticated machines lined one wall of the room. Only one of the men in the heavy decontamination suits remained inside.

The man removed the last straps from Small's body. It was slow work with the suit's thick gloves.

"Am I contagious or something?" Small asked.

"There was always that possibility," the man replied. "Not so much now, though. Our preliminary tests show you're probably clean."

Tests? What tests? Small decided not to ask too many questions before he knew which way the wind blew.

"However, I'd like to check you out a bit just to make sure. If you could sit up, please, and swing your legs over the side of the gurney?"

Small did as he was told. The rest of the examination seemed like a standard physical exam. Small was instructed to cough now and then, and to open wide for a look down the throat and to tilt his head for the light in the ears. Some of the instruments the fellow used looked a little strange. But besides a couple of the metal objects feeling a bit too cold against his skin, nothing hurt.

Small decided he could risk starting a conversation. "You're acting like this is standard procedure."

"It is something we need to do from time to time," his examiner replied as he continued to poke and prod. "All sorts of people and things try to use any means possible to get at Wolfram and Hart every day. We just try to make it a little more difficult for them to succeed."

"Get at? I certainly—"

The other man smiled behind his faceplate. "I don't mean to imply that you were making such an attempt. Of course there will be the standard investigation, but most of these interlopers try to sneak by our sensors. I'm here to make sure they don't succeed." He tapped Small on the shoulder. "You are here because you were touched by a demon."

Touched? Yeah, especially by the creature's slime. Small nodded, but didn't say anything.

"It has subtly changed your signature."

"You mean how I sign my name?"

"Nothing so simple." The examiner glanced at a computer monitor in the corner of the room. "Our detection equipment is state-of-the-art." He punched a series of commands, then nodded, satisfied, as the results appeared on the monitor. "It seems a bit of the demon has stayed with you. Sort of like a fingerprint on your soul."

Small's escort sat down on the room's only chair and took a moment to remove his headgear. The helmet came off with a hiss of air.

The man inside had a lean face with close-cropped gray hair. He looked to Small like he might be ex-military.

"Maybe this will make it more comfortable to talk. Please describe what happened."

Small recounted the whole incident with Phil, or at least the thing that had looked like Phil.

The other man nodded. "Exactly as I suspected. They're looking for a way to infiltrate the firm."

"They?"

"They've left their imprint on you with a first contact. We should be able to remove the connection. That will allow you to go back out in the field." He leaned over and checked the monitor again. "And to answer your earlier question: No, you're not contagious."

Small heard a soft beep. The other man fingered an earpiece Small hadn't noticed before.

"One of your superiors wants to talk to you. So I guess we're done for now."

His examiner got up from his chair, grabbing his headgear. The door opened as he approached.

The higher-ups wanted him? Had Small screwed up enough to demand the attention of Lilah Morgan?

The other man smiled as he passed through the door. "You can stay right here."

The door sealed again behind him. So Small would now wait for the next round of inquisitors. It felt a bit like those times he had gotten on the wrong side of Internal Affairs, back in his cop days. Except the IA guys had only wanted his badge.

The door hissed back open only a moment later. Small was surprised to realize that he was both relieved and disappointed to see that it wasn't Lilah who had come to see him, but her assistant, David. The relief came because he was a little scared of Lilah, the disappointment because he thought he merited more than a lowly assistant.

"Grady," David began. "Glad to see you're okay." Somehow, David looked more annoyed than pleased. "So, I've read the report on the incident. We hired you because you have a reputation. You're a man of action. You get the job done. Well, you've already got yourself right in the middle of some very big action."

"Right in the middle?" Why was Small asking the questions?

"Your encounter with the demon has marked you, I understand."

"Oh, that. The 'fingerprint on the soul' stuff. They said they'd fix me right up."

"Oh, I don't think so." David smiled at last. "You encountered a rare and powerful creature. Part of a small group, from what I understand. We want to lure them in so we can find a way to use them. And you're going to be our point man."

So they weren't going to get this fingerprint thing out of him? He didn't like the sound of that at all. "Does Ms. Morgan know about this?" he asked.

"Let's not bother her until we have something of substance to report." David shook his head. "You're well paid, Mr. Small. Now you're going to be well-paid bait." David turned to leave the room.

"Bait?" Small echoed.

"But don't worry," David called over his shoulder. "You are a valuable asset. Wolfram and Hart will be behind you all the way."

Angel noticed the difference as soon as he stepped through the door. The atmosphere in the hotel had changed completely. Everybody was all smiles.

Angel thought he'd rarely seen such a happy homecoming. Especially before a crisis ended.

"Hey there, big guy!" Lorne called as soon as he had walked in. "Do me a favor and give me a few bars of 'New York, New York'!"

"Uh," Angel started his shaky version in reply. "You mean, 'If you can make it there, you can make it anywhere'?"

"Good enough!" Lorne grimaced, then grinned. "He's the real deal!"

"Angel!" Cordy cried as he walked down the stairs. "I'm glad you're safe."

Angel grinned back at her. It was nice to know she was still concerned for him. Before all her recent problems with the Higher Powers, he had thought that he and Cordy might have a future together.

"But how about the other me? Did you get anything out of him?" Gunn asked. "Or maybe you kicked his ass so I don't have to worry about him anymore?"

"Not that much kicking." Angel shrugged. "A little, maybe. But I found out a thing or two. I followed him back to the demons' lair."

Wesley nodded. "Makes sense. They have a hidden base of operation?"

"In an old warehouse, about thirty blocks from here. When I walked in, they were all chanting, like the middle of some ritual."

"Were there seven of them?" Wesley asked.

Angel was surprised he knew. "Well, yeah."

"Excellent." The former Watcher glanced down at the book in front of him. "They didn't happen to have some sort of crystal with them, by any chance? Perhaps involved in the ritual? A glowing crystal, fairly large, much like the color of the sea?

"Um, yeah. There was a crystal. Actually, I thought it was more like—lime green."

"Close enough, I imagine. These old books get a

tad poetic on occasion." Wesley glanced down once more. "Did you see them in their natural state? That would have happened during the ritual, certainly. They looked rather like a bunch of rocks, piled in human form?"

"Uh—yeah?"

"And did anything come out of the crystal? Especially after you roughed up one or two of them?"

"You did rough 'em up, didn't you?" Gunn urged.

It was Angel's turn to shake his head. "I've got the feeling you can tell me. You've figured out what these things are, huh?"

"Apparently so," Wesley agreed.

Angel felt like everyone already knew the punch line to his new joke. So much for his dangerous night of discovery. Well, he knew plenty of details Wesley would never find in one of his books. In fact, he thought one of those details was particularly important. "Did you know one of them hopped a cab to Wolfram and Hart?" he asked.

Wesley raised his eyebrows in surprise as he shook his head.

Angel folded his arms in triumph. "I didn't think so."

"That could mean a number of different things," Wesley said.

"Like the demons are working for the lawyers?" Lorne ventured. "What else is new?"

"Possibly," Wesley replied, some doubt in his voice. "Wolfram and Hart tend to be more subtle than that—usually. These demons are running around, barging in on people, waving guns in broad daylight. Not Wolfram and Hart's style." Wesley patted the book in front of him. "But we've gotten to know a couple of important things. These demons you were roughing up—did any of them breathe on you?"

Angel shook his head. "That, I already knew enough about—thanks to all that stuff with Gunn and Fred. They sure tried a couple of times. I was too fast on my feet. Didn't stay in one spot long enough to share the air."

"And did you rough up any of them enough for them to"—Wesley paused—"disincorporate?"

"You mean the way they melted?" Angel asked.

Gunn looked like he'd eaten something bad. "That messy liquid stuff."

"And what happened next?" Wesley urged.

"Well, it's like you just started to say, I think. The things are fairly easy to fight. I threw one guy who looked like a cop against the wall, and he just went kind of squishy. But a moment later he was pulled back together, just above that green crystal."

"As I suspected." Wesley tapped his fingers on the open page. "When we stopped these things the other times, we weren't killing them. We were just . . . inconveniencing them for a little while."

"So what now?"

"Well, I think I can name our demons," he said with a hint of pride. Wesley was never so happy as when he could put a name to something. "We are looking at the Seven Sinners, a group of demons who want to bring about something called"—Wesley ran his finger along the page—"ah . . . the Great Remorse."

Angel frowned. "That doesn't sound good."

"Do any of these ever sound good?" Gunn asked.

Angel glanced down at the open book in front of Wesley. The page featured a woodcut of a demon made of rock that looked a little like the creatures he had seen. "At least we know what we're up against. Don't we?"

"We are up against quite a bit. The Seven Sinners are very particular about whom they choose to imitate."

"So we didn't just stumble into this?" Fred asked. "They were looking for us?"

"Probably ever since they came to our dimension. In fact, they may have come to this particular town specifically to find us. They are extremely sensitive to the way people are connected, and first found someone who only had a trace connection with their ultimate goal."

"Really?" Cordy asked. "They could have just looked us up in the phone book."

Wesley shook his head. "The only thing they can

read—at least when they're in rock form—are auras. And they read those so they can steal them."

"Let me see if I've got this," Angel said. "So they find traces of . . . say . . . Phil, who's done business with us—or of someone maybe even more removed, like, say, somebody who talked to Phil's best friend's landlord, and then they hunt for Phil from there?"

"So they can get to us," Wesley agreed.

"It's like the 'six degrees of Kevin Bacon,'" Cordy added. "Everybody's connected to everybody else—eventually."

Lorne nodded. "Yes, except this chain probably doesn't include Cher. Although, come to think of it, that demon double business could explain a lot of her later career."

"So we've got a problem with the Seven Sinners," Angel replied. "What's their final goal?"

"Their first goal is to reach the proper persons who will be involved with their final goal: those critical souls who will lead to the Remorse. They take over their lives, then destroy the original.

"Let me read you a bit from this book," Wesley continued:

"'Some ancient scholars hold that demons were spawned in a dimension of exiled souls. Souls cast aside to relive the agony of lives spent in moral missteps.

"'After decades of incontinence, these carnal

sinners of excess, deprivation, and minor depravities realized their lives were wasted. They were then forced to relive with shame their regrettable behavior.

"'The Seven Sinners proliferated and grew fat on this pain.

"'The continuous flow of new exiles could not keep pace with the Sinners' appetite. In order to survive, the demons fled this dimension to discover another where they might find and suck dry any other that supported a surfeit of remorse.

"'Over time, a myth developed that the Seven Sinners emerged from the dimension called Purgatory.'"

"I'm liking these guys even less," Gunn remarked.

"They are powerful and ancient beings," Wesley replied. "Destroying their true selves—the original of the body they have assumed—gives the doubles power, which in turn helps to bring about the Remorse."

"What you're saying is," Gunn ventured, "the more of us they kill, the easier it will be for them to kill the rest of us?"

"Something like that. But they have a greater goal as well. And that goal is right in this room."

Wesley nodded at Angel.

"We know that Angel is the subject of more than one prophecy." Wesley didn't add that he had been fooled by one such false prophecy concerning Angel, almost destroying them all. "I think these very prophecies are what attracted the Sinners.

"We know that Wolfram and Hart is also very interested in something in Angel's future. Something cataclysmic. I'd say Angel was the Seven Sinners' eventual goal. These demons are looking forward to an apocalypse."

"What do you mean—'eventual goal'?" Fred asked.

"Well, of course they'll double him, and then destroy him, just like the rest of us. But they are looking for something more." Wesley paused to look at everybody in the room.

"You've noticed, perhaps, that the Sinners reproduce our most negative aspects."

Angel laughed a bit at that. "I was worried that the demons who came from Fred and Gunn might know too many of my moves. But then, instead of taking me on, they started fighting among themselves."

"Exactly," Wesley agreed. "It is somewhere in that fact that I think we might find their weakness, and our salvation. The demons twist the personalities of the originals. According to my research, they do the same to the original prophecy. They want to control the apocalypse and make it into their own."

"So they make the apocalypse worse?" Lorne said with a frown. "Is that even possible?"

"Well, their apocalypse puts the Seven Sinners in control."

Lorne nodded. "Point taken."

"All this fighting among themselves," Angel asked. "Does it give us more of a chance?"

It was Wesley's turn to nod. "They will squabble among themselves, at least at first. Which leads to my other finding. They've picked Angel for another reason. They are looking for a leader, strong and cunning. The sort who can assert his authority over the worst scum in demonkind.

"They're looking for Angelus."

CHAPTER ELEVEN

"Mr. Manchester?"

He felt like he was crawling up out of a deep pit.

He saw a haze of light. He grunted. It was far too bright. He squinted, waiting for the world to come into focus.

"He's awake."

He lay in a hospital room. A doctor peered down over him, and a couple of toughs who looked like plainclothes cops flanked either side of the bed. Which meant he was still alive. Either that, or God had a very weird sense of humor.

Somehow, Gunn and Fred had saved his bacon.

The doctor looked over his shoulder.

"Can he talk?" one of the other men asked. Both of the plainclothes were beefy, with sports coats that looked a little the worse for wear. They were definitely cops.

"Not right away. Give him a little time. He's probably still pretty disoriented."

Phil pulled his lips apart. His throat was very dry.

"Here. Take a little water." The doctor offered him a plastic bottle with a straw.

Water never tasted so good.

Phil took a deep breath. That was better. He swallowed. He had one thing he needed to say. "Ang—," he started. "Angel." His voice was hoarse. It sounded like it was coming from very far away. He closed his eyes. He wondered if he'd been out for a while. He felt like he could go right back to sleep.

"I think it was a mistake to bring you in here," the doctor was saying to the others. "He's still very weak. This may have to wait until later."

Phil opened his eyes again. While all these people were here, he had to make the effort. "Call . . . call Angel. Angel Investigations. They'll know what to do."

"Angel?" the doctor said.

"Those are the folks who brought him in," one of the cops explained. I understand the nursing staff has instructions to call them once he wakes up."

"It sounds like you know the nurses better than I do," the doctor said with a slight smile. "I think it may be a little premature to allow too many people to visit. Maybe when Mr. Manchester is a little stronger. Don't worry. Let's let him get a bit more sleep. Soon you'll be able to talk just as much as you want."

One of the cops looked past the doctor. "Mr. Manchester. We need to ask you some questions about your assailant. We'll let your friends know you're okay, even tell them you'd like a visit. But first give us time to let the L.A.P.D. do its job."

"You've said what you needed to," the doctor replied. "Now let my patient get some rest."

All three of them left the room.

Phil feared this job was completely beyond the L.A.P.D.'s expertise.

But the doctor was right. He needed to sleep.

They worked together for the Remorse.

They used the best strengths of their human hosts. They had but a single purpose. But six of the Seven did not have the tools.

He knew how to do it best. The rest were just fools.

Now he was Grady Small. And more than Grady Small. He had chosen the perfect vessel to succeed. His memories were those of a Los Angeles policeman, and a man who knew how to twist the rules to get what he wanted. His skills were exactly what they needed to succeed. He knew how to use authority. They'd learn that he should be the leader.

Yet the others resisted him. The one called

Gunn thought that Gunn was the better fighter, the one called Fred thought Grady Small didn't have the brains.

He would show them.

The new Grady Small fingered the piece he'd stolen, an exact match for the gun the original—the inferior, human Grady Small—wore in his shoulder holster. A nice, warm .38. That was all the brains he needed.

He would show them all.

He hated that he had to hesitate—that the Sinners, in their worship of the Remorse, were called back to the Stone once in every day, forced to work together in their original form. Their new personalities were suppressed as they worked to bring new vessels into the fold. But a bit of his new vessel stuck with this Sinner, and showed him the truth. He watched the others through the eyes of Grady Small. Mouthed the words with them, only now realizing how little they meant. The Great Remorse would never come from words. It would come from will. Never had he realized the others were so weak!

Weak, yes. But not all of them were blind.

He had convinced the one who had taken on the form of Phil Manchester to work with him. Grady Small knew the police. He would find a way into the hospital. He would allow the Sinner Phil to confront his human original, and to kill him as was ordained. Their power would bring the human Small under their control, and the Sinner would kill his double and be fulfilled. Together they would bring down all before them.

And the others would realize who should be the leader, the greatest of the Sinners, Lord of the Remorse.

He left the others behind when the ritual was finally over, taking a cab to the hospital.

He told the Sinner Phil to wait for his signal. Of course, he would have to revert to his true form for an instant in order to commune with another of his kind, but that should not prove to be a problem. There were many deserted corners in a hospital at night.

He went up to the floor where they were keeping the real Phil Manchester. It was a surgical floor, probably where they had put Phil right after they had removed the bullets. They had placed him in a private room in a quiet corner of the ward. Slightly out of the way, easy to guard, just out of sight of the nurses' station—it must have seemed perfect to the police. It was good enough for the new Grady Small to do his job as well.

He saw two cops talking. He knew the way these stakeouts worked. One cop would be inside the room, the other guarding the door from the hallway. Their superiors weren't taking any chances with this one. It was by the book. Small shook his head. It was certainly better police work than he was used to. For a lesser being than the new Grady Small, it might have been too much.

Ah. Grady Small had been cut a break. His human self had known one of these guys. A uniformed cop named Stan. His human self had bought Stan a beer or two, too, back in the day. This Grady Small could not be stopped. Already, he could see the way. He sidled over to the nurses' station. Only one woman behind the desk, engrossed in her computer.

Small took in the counter before him. He saw a stack of patient charts in one corner. He quietly moved next to the pile and lifted the top file. The second folder was labeled PHIL MANCHESTER.

So easy. His path was clear. Nothing could stop him now.

The doctor had placed a NO VISITORS restriction. It was noted in bright red, right at the top of the chart. So neither the new Fred nor the new Gunn could come in just yet. He would rather not use them, anyway. He'd show them which one among their number held the true "brains."

The two cops stopped talking—they were ending their break—and the guy he'd known sat down in his chair just outside the door. The other guy disappeared inside the room. The Lords of the Remorse smiled upon him. For Grady Small, there was no such word as "failure."

"Hey, Stan!" he called to the cop in front of the room.

"Grady!" Stan looked up and said with a smile. But the smile slipped a little bit as he added, "What are you doing here?"

"I've got a sick aunt two floors down," Small replied. "I heard you guys had Phil Manchester up here. That's one hell of a case, huh? I thought so long as I was here, I'd come up and see what really happened. I may be retired from the force, but the old cop curiosity never quits."

Stan shook his head, crossing his arms in front of him. "Sorry, Grady. Nobody goes inside. Besides, I thought you hated Phil."

Grady Small laughed at that. "Sure, there was no love lost between us. But no guy deserves to be shot point-blank. I figured I'd find out what I could here, then see what I could dig up on the street."

"Once a cop, always a cop, huh? You should be glad you're not on the force anymore. This is a flat-out, boring detail. But someone with the chief's ear wants this guy watched." Stan sighed. "There're too many people in a place like this for anyone to try anything. All we do here is sit and stare at the walls."

"Yeah," Small agreed with a laugh. "I can remember those assignments. Eight hours of working hard, just waiting." He waved back down the hall. "Listen, you want anything? I'd be glad to get you a sandwich or something. You need to use the john? I could spell you out here for a minute." He jerked his thumb toward the lone nurse at the station. "This place has less action than Forest Lawn. Take a break. Who'd know?"

Stan kept his seat. "Nah. Somehow the chief would find out. The chief always finds out. The guy's eyes have got eyes." He frowned up at the man he thought he knew. "Look, Grady. I'm probably talking to you too long as it is. This case is too important to the brass downtown. We have strict orders to keep the patient under constant observation and be in regular contact with both the nursing station and the boys downtown. You gotta do what you gotta do. No one's going to get by us."

Small nodded in what he thought looked like sympathy. So this would take a little longer. But the new Grady Small had more resources than simple deception.

Nothing would stop his victory.

He reached deep within the new Grady Small for the ancient gift of the Sinners, the agent of change. "Okay, you can't leave. But can I show you something?" He dug deep into his coat pocket.

"You got something choice?" Stan glanced guiltily toward the nurses' station, but then smiled up at Small.

Grady Small had a reputation around the squad

room. Whenever he got back from a vice raid, he always kept a few samples.

"I got something you won't believe. Let's take this someplace private."

He walked a few paces around the corner. Stan got out of his chair and followed him. He motioned the cop a little farther forward, making sure Stan leaned away from the nurses' station, so they were both hidden by a wall.

There was nothing in his pocket but a wadded-up piece of tissue paper. It would be enough. Grady Small would triumph.

He allowed the Sinner within him to emerge, his face turning hard and sharp for an instant.

"Grady? What the hell—"

The Greatest Sinner of All freed the seeds of creation. They sparkled as they surrounded their newest vessel.

The cop choked in surprise. "What is that stuff? Who are you? What are you?" He swiped at the mist as if he might wave it away.

But it was already too late. The substance of the Remorse had sampled his soul. Soon, his double would arrive to dispose of him and take his place. It would be simple to reach Phil after that.

They were one step closer to the Remorse.

Grady Small turned and quickly walked away while the cop was still startled, bypassing the elevators, jumping down the stairs three at a time. He heard no sounds of pursuit. He stepped out of the stairwell three floors down, and quietly took an elevator down to the laundry room in the basement.

This room was empty this time of night.

He lay down inside a big, empty laundry cart. No one would bother him here. He let his essence shift, became the Sinner of stone that was his natural state, and signaled the others when to come.

Great would be the Remorse, and he would be greatest of all.

They had killed thirteen times since they had come to this city, had added the strength of thirteen life-forms into their own. They would kill at least seven more, perhaps absorbing the energy of three times seven, a most powerful and fitting number.

They approached their true power at last.

The strength from each conquered life never lasted long enough. But it would last forever once they reached their goal. The Sinners would be supreme, and all would bow, or die, before the power of the Remorse.

The thing that looked like Grady Small lay quiet in the laundry cart and waited.

Angel had to find a way to protect all of them from these things. Angel needed to make plans.

"We need to bring Connor in here. He's out on his own. He knows nothing about the Sinners. He's the most vulnerable of all of us."

Cordy shook her head. "I gave him a phone. He's not answering it."

Angel sighed. He was probably just as good at electronics as his old man.

She stood up from her desk and grabbed her purse. "Maybe I'd better go out there and pick him up in person. I think he trusts me as much as anybody here."

He started to object, until he realized that Cordy was right.

If he was to go and demand Connor's return, as likely as not the two of them would get into a fight. A painful, time-consuming fight, allowing the Seven Sinners to do whatever they would with the rest of his crew.

Two of his people were already in danger. He wanted to make sure nobody else was added to the list.

"She's right," he agreed. "It would be fastest."

"Should Cordy go alone?" Fred asked. "I could go along. Or maybe Gunn could keep her company."

Wesley shook his head. "That might be even more dangerous. The demons have a connection to their doubles. If we send one of those who's already been affected, it may actually attract the demons, and lead them right to the affected party—and Connor."

And, Angel thought, *Connor really didn't trust*

139

anybody in his crew except Cordy. He didn't want to ask the next question, but felt he had to. "What if they've already gotten to Connor?"

"I'd be the one to ask about that," Lorne volunteered. "I'll keep Cordy company. Hey, it's dark. I'll wear a hat."

Cordy looked sharply at him. "I'll need to talk to Connor alone."

"Understood. But I'll be waiting just down the hall. And if there's any problem, we'll get Connor to sing."

"All right," Angel said to both of them. "Go now. Take a cab. Get back here as soon as you can. And be careful. You know how to use a cell phone."

Cordy smiled. "I was using a phone before I knew how to talk. But I bet most of you already knew that."

"Hey, I've got a phone, too, and I know how to use it," Lorne chirped in. "This place is *numero uno* on my speed-dial."

Angel smiled slightly. "So we'll be expecting your call. Now get out of here." At least, he thought, he could pick up the phone when they called him. What was "speed-dial," anyway?

"So what's next for the rest of us?" he asked Fred, Gunn, and Wesley as Cordy and Lorne walked out the door.

"We need to know where the demons will strike next," Wesley said. "They'd want to get us alone.

140

Maybe change one or more of us without the others knowing."

"Well, we'll just have to keep our distance from newcomers until Lorne runs his next sing-a-thon."

"And we have to remember," Wesley added, "that some of them think like us."

"On a really bad day, maybe," Gunn replied.

"I'm sorry, guys," Fred said, stifling a yawn. "I feel like I have to rest."

"I don't think that's entirely your fault," Wesley replied. "From my reading, I believe the demons might drain off some energy as well as a piece of the soul."

"So these creeps are going to steal our energy, too?" Gunn said with a groan. "Nothing but good news."

"So where else are we vulnerable?" Angel asked.

"Has the hospital called?" Fred interrupted as she wearily climbed the stairs. "I worry about Phil."

The noise woke him. Someone grunted. Something banged against the wall.

Phil opened his eyes to see two men, struggling.

They were both the same police officer, dressed in identical blue.

Nowhere was safe from these demon doubles. They had found a way to get to him.

Phil struggled to sit up. He was strapped to all

sorts of tubes and wires. And he felt like he had no strength at all.

Shouldn't there be a call button around here somewhere? No doubt they would have pointed it out to him if he had been awake long enough to listen.

One cop pushed the other against a folding tray table. It collapsed with a crash. Wouldn't they hear that out in the nurses' station?

Phil tried to shout, but his throat was so dry that he barely made a sound. He had no strength. He could barely move. Unless he could find some way to contact somebody outside this room, he imagined he was watching the lead-up to his own death.

One of the cops pulled out a blade, a wicked bowie knife kind of thing, with a serrated edge. The sort of thing you'd bring if you were planning to kill someone without a lot of noise.

Phil was guessing that the cop with the knife was a demon.

The other cop tried to push the knife arm away, but the double swung the knife under the real cop's guard, past his elbow, between the ribs. The real cop grunted in pain and surprise.

The demon stabbed him again and again and again. Blood poured from half a dozen wounds. The policeman fell over. He stopped moving.

The human was dead.

A green glow settled over the remaining double.

The demon's eyes pulsed with an inner light. He raised both arms, fists clenched, toward the ceiling. "Yes! We are one step closer to the Remorse."

The glow faded. The demon turned to Phil. "And you have been honored to witness the event. This is only the beginning. It's time for you to have some more direct participation."

The demon's visage shifted for an instant to a face made of piled stones. "I believe you'll know both of our new arrivals."

Phil heard a knock on the door.

"Come in," the cop demon said pleasantly.

Phil saw himself walk into the room; himself and an overfed, corrupt cop by the name of Grady Small. He doubted, though, that the Grady Small in front of him was any more human than the Phil Manchester by his side.

"I need your help." The uniformed demon nodded to his dead double. "Let's put him out of the way."

The three of them pushed the body into the closet. Phil knew they wouldn't need to hide it for long.

As he turned to watch them hide the corpse, he noticed a bright red button on the table next to his head. The call button, so close that even he could reach it. He waited until the three of them showed their backs to him, and punched it with his thumb.

"The cop's body needs to be found here," Grady

Small said as he closed the closet door. "That's part of our plan. You, of course, will still be in bed. Or your double will, on the way to a miraculous recovery, just in time to meet whoever shows up from Angel Investigations. And then we take them, too."

He pointed with his thumb toward the door. "Your real body's going out in that laundry basket in the hall."

"Why bother explaining any of this rubbish?" the other Phil demanded. "Let's kill the punter now. I don't like to be kept waiting."

Grady Small grinned at the demon by his side. He looked down at the real Phil Manchester. "Were you ever this impatient? Sorry, Phil, but we need your energy."

"You're being sacrificed for something of much greater value than your pitiful life," his double said with a sneer. He nodded to Small. "I would like to use that knife now."

Small frowned at that. "A pillow would be far neater."

"You're right. I would have liked to see the blood, though."

"Is there something wrong here?" a woman's voice asked sharply. "What are all of you doing in the room?"

Grady Small spun to greet her. "Good to see you, Nurse. Mr. Manchester seems a little upset. I'll be out in the hall for a minute."

The nurse was here. The call button had worked.

"Nurse!" he shouted. "Get these men out of the room."

The nurse frowned. "Mr. Manchester?"

"They're trying to kill me!"

The nurse's frown deepened. "These are the police, Mr. Manchester. They're here to protect you."

They would, Phil thought, *if they were really the police.* How could he get her to understand?

He pointed at the demon in uniform. "But he had a knife. He killed the other cop."

"Other cop?" the demon replied with a grin. "Ernie went downstairs to get a couple cups of coffee."

"No, another cop, looked just like him!"

"What are you talking about?" the demon asked. "How could I be dead? I'm standing right here, Phil."

The nurse made a *tut-tut* sound. "When you've been through the sort of trauma you have, Mr. Manchester, it can make you think you see all sorts of things." She glanced at the cop. "Maybe I'd better give him something to help him sleep."

"Sounds like it's for the best," Small said sympathetically.

The cop. He was the only one here, when a moment ago there had been three. Small had left the room. Where had the other Phil gone? He noticed the door to the bathroom was closed. If the nurse saw another man who looked just like him, she'd have to believe Phil's story.

"But there were three of them in here," Phil insisted. "One of them looked like me! He's hiding—"

The nurse shook her head. "I'm sure it's all very upsetting. You'll feel much better once you've had a little rest." She shot a full syringe into the tubes feeding his intravenous solutions. "You have to be alert in the morning. That's when the investigating detectives are coming back."

"That's right, Mr. Manchester. You don't want to disappoint those guys."

He wasn't going to be alive to talk to the investigating detectives. But how could he get the nurse to believe him? The bathroom! She had to look in the bathroom.

"There'ss anotthherr . . . ," he began. His voice sounded strange and far away. His eyes wanted to close. "Batthroom."

"You're still fitted with a catheter, Mr. Manchester. That shouldn't be a problem. Let me know if you need to use the bedpan." She smiled at the demon cop. "Now we need to let him get his rest."

"Yeah," the cop said as she went out the door. "I'll make sure he isn't disturbed."

Grady Small stepped back in the room as the

nurse departed. He rapped sharply on the bath-room door. "Let's get this party started."

The other Phil stepped back into the room, all smiles. "I think my rotter double tried to give the game away."

"Yeah," the cop agreed. "Too bad he's delusional."

Phil fought to keep his eyes open. Why? What difference did it make? He guessed he wanted to be awake for his own demise.

His double stepped to the edge of the bed. "You're a goner. But take a look, Mr. Philip Manchester, at your legacy."

Phil watched the other preen through half-closed eyelids. God, his double was full of himself. Did Phil ever sound like that?

"That's right. Take a final look at me. A little reward before we take your life-energy. You led us to our final goal. Your pitiful little career as a private investigator, barely scraping by on bottom-of-the-barrel divorce cases, lost loved ones, crap cases that barely paid. And how about that immigration scam?"

Phil wasn't proud of that one. His partners at the time hadn't told him the whole story. When he'd found out what was really going on, they'd tried to kill him.

The demon Phil grinned as he pulled a pillow from behind the real thing's head. This guy was him—sort of—and knew every pimple on his career.

"You're not losing much. You barely had a life to begin with. Your death will finally fuel something that matters!"

The new Phil started to giggle.

"We are surrounded by power," Grady Small announced. "The Remorse is near!"

Phil heard something else. A scuffle of some sort. Were the demons fighting? His eyes kept closing.

"No," Grady Small shouted. "You will not stop me! This is my destiny!"

He forced his eyes open.

The uniformed cop was falling apart—literally, turning from flesh to flash of stone, then melting into a thick, yellow liquid. The other Phil was cowering in the corner. He guessed that Grady Small was just a puddle on the floor.

"Hey, Phil!" a voice called from the doorway. "I understand you were looking forward to a visit!" Two figures stood there. They both waved.

Angel and Gunn were all smiles as they closed the door and walked over to the bed.

CHAPTER TWELVE

Wesley found himself alone in his old haunts. Angel and Gunn had gone to rescue Phil from the hospital, while Cordy and Lorne were in the middle of bringing Connor back into the fold. Fred was taking a nap, and had asked to be woken in an hour.

So it was just Wesley Wyndam-Pryce and the old hotel. He guessed Angel and the others were beginning to trust him again. Either that, or they were too busy to care.

He had spent dozens of late nights in this lobby, researching one supernatural threat after another. He was surprised at how much he missed the place. There was something very reassuring about this hotel's mix of art deco and natural wood, the high ceilings, the thick carpeting, the quiet charm. This place had stood for three quarters of a century, an eternity in the up-to-the-minute world of Los Angeles. The Hyperion Hotel had stood the test of time. It had given Wesley and the others a sense that maybe they could persevere against the forces of darkness.

Sometime soon, perhaps after Fred awoke, he needed to fetch more reference materials from his apartment. Now that he had identified the evil they faced, he could research how others had dealt with similar problems. And he had a second reason to leave the hotel. He needed a conference with someone who would not be too welcome here.

Not that he was concerned about Lilah. A demon might have been headed toward her law firm, but Wolfram & Hart had resources far beyond anything around here. And he still couldn't believe the firm was working with these particular demons. If Wolfram & Hart were going to destroy the world, they'd do it on their own terms, thank you. But one way or another—sometimes he learned more through the subjects Lilah *wouldn't* talk about—she would tell him what he needed to know.

He still had to get in touch with her. He fished his own phone out of his pocket to keep the line at the hotel free. He dialed her direct line.

"Wesley!" she replied as soon as she read his caller ID. "What a pleasant surprise."

"Something's come up. We need to talk."

"Do we?" Sometimes, her amused voice could

be really infuriating. "You must be talking about the latest demon infestation. I understand you're back working with Angel on that."

And he was worried that she might not know about something. Still, he supposed he should pass on his information.

"I have it on good authority that one of those demons was headed straight for your headquarters."

"They've already tried to compromise one of our operatives. Not that it's gotten them very far. But I can't really talk here. We need to go somewhere more private if we're going to exchange any information."

"Exchange information? Most certainly."

"The usual place? In two hours?"

"Two hours? Done."

Wesley turned off the phone. Perhaps this wasn't the wisest course of action. But he felt he needed to use every resource available if he was going to defeat these things. He and Lilah might be on opposite sides of the great conflict, yet they had helped each other more than once when it had suited their mutual needs.

After all, Lilah didn't want the world to end any more than he did. And these were world-ending demons, he was quite sure of that.

And it sounded like Lilah and those she worked for were threatened by these things as well. That meant she might be a bit more truthful. But Wolfram & Hart always wanted to hold on to the winning hand. Wesley just hoped he could get Lilah to tell him enough. And that the other members of Angel Investigations could remain safe until he got that information.

Phil saw his other self backed into a corner.

"Maybe we can keep this one alive," Angel mused.

"You mean at least long enough to question him?" Gunn replied.

Phil's double spat on the floor before them. "Not bloody likely. No matter how many times you have your little victories, we will win in the end. We will feed on every soul upon this planet, until the whole world is nothing but a withered husk."

"So you'll destroy everyone here?" Angel asked.

"Doesn't sound very friendly," Gunn agreed. "What's in it for you?"

The demon shrugged. "We move on to the next world. We have so many dimensions on which to feed."

"Watch it!" Gunn called as the creature lunged for Angel. But Angel had already moved elsewhere. The glittering mist the demon had spread before it hung in the empty air.

The demon screamed and launched itself back at Gunn. Gunn met it with a roundhouse kick.

Phil winced as he heard something snap inside the demon.

"There is no way you can stop us!" the thing screamed as it dissolved into a puddle on the floor.

"Oh, there's a way," Angel said as he watched the puddle disappear. "There's always a way."

He shrugged when he saw the other two waiting for an explanation. "Well, at least until now."

"Hey, guys." Phil was never so happy to see anybody in his life. He sat up as far as he could in bed. Some of his energy seemed to be coming back. He guessed that was what a little adrenaline could do for you. "Thanks for saving my life."

"Hospitals can be dangerous places," Gunn agreed. "So they were going to kill you—"

"And take my place. Yeah. That much, I figured out."

Angel pointed at the floor, empty save for a fallen tray table. "Nice of them to remove the evidence."

"Not all the evidence. There's a dead cop in the closet."

"A dead cop?" Gunn frowned. "Maybe we should be going. I don't think they'll attack you again tonight. Especially with a body here and all."

"So nobody saw you come in?" Phil asked.

They both looked slightly offended.

"Please, Phil," Angel said. "Do you think anybody knows we're in here?"

"Yeah, why should they worry? There's a cop in

153

here with you at all times." Gunn glanced toward the closet. "Of course, the cop happens to be dead."

"They'll probably triple the guard on you after this. There'll be too many for the demons to get to you." Angel took a step toward the hall to listen at the doorway. "I think we've still got a minute. Tell us what you know about the case. We'll fill you in from our end."

Phil was only too happy to oblige. "I saw one of the demons kill his double. It was the cop. He was knifed right in front of me. I'm surprised there isn't more blood on the floor. Anyway, the demon seemed to become positively giddy with energy. Oh, and I've been to where they hide."

"The warehouse?" Angel asked. "I followed them there, too, and saw some weird ritual with the crystal."

Phil smiled at that. "Ah, but did you try to touch the crystal? That's when things got interesting. Very touchy they are about that. I think that glowing rock's both their source of strength and their Achilles' heel."

Angel frowned. Phil could hear voices coming in from the hall.

"Yeah," Angel replied, "we gotta go." He waved to Phil. "Once you feel a little better, we want you in on this."

Phil continued to grin. "Does it pay anything?"

"Does it pay anything?" Angel looked slightly offended. "We're saving the world from a hideous evil."

"Doesn't pay one red cent," Gunn added. "Business as usual at Angel Investigations."

"Well, I guess I might owe you guys a favor. I'm in. We'll make 'em sorry they ever messed with the likes of us."

"Let's hope so, Phil." Angel opened the door and took a look outside. He waved for Gunn to follow. "I think it's time for the authorities to take over."

He closed the door behind them as they moved silently into the hall.

David wouldn't let this thing alone.

At least, Small thought, he was free of that sealed room with all its strange machines and examination instruments. But Small had been released into David's custody and was told to stay with the man until given further orders.

"Don't worry. We're going to take every precaution." David had been saying things like that ever since they had left the medical room.

Small had given up responding to his superior. Why did Small have so much trouble believing this guy?

"I don't think they're very bright." The young man slapped Small on the shoulder. "We can use them. This firm has a lot of experience in this sort of thing.

"It was so simple too. Your demon double came right to Wolfram and Hart. I intercepted it before it could even get close to the inner censors."

Small sighed. The way this was going, David would stumble right into the middle of something and get them both killed.

"Did it do anything to you?" Small asked. "They do this spray thing—"

"It wouldn't dare. It wants my cooperation. Offered me good money to get you alone."

"And you agreed?"

"Hey, I always like to make a little money on the side." David laughed. "I tell you, Grady, you can't take a joke."

Not when it was at his expense. He also didn't like twerps calling him by his first name.

"I think we need to bring Ms. Morgan in on this," Small insisted.

"Oh we will, we will." David kept on grinning. "But how much better would it be if we could give her something when we do talk to her?"

It occurred to Small then just why he was losing this argument. "You want to get the credit for this, don't you? Catching a demon all by yourself? Use it to move up in the company?"

"Ah, I see you know the way things work. Not so different with the cops, I imagine."

Well, the cops at least liked to keep up the appearance of doing the right thing. But he didn't bother explaining anything more to this idiot.

Instead, he announced, "Well, I don't work here unless I go through channels." He pulled out the business card his real boss had given him, with instructions to call her day or night, and quickly punched the number into his cell phone.

"This is Lilah Morgan. I will be out of the office for the next few hours. Please leave a message. If this is an emergency, please call—"

Small frowned. This wasn't exactly an emergency, more like a disagreement with an idiot. He flipped the phone closed. He would try her again before they got into the thick of things.

David chuckled. "He thinks he's gonna pull one over on us." He nodded to Small. "Wait until we catch one of these things. The senior partners will really take notice of me then!"

Small didn't like that reference at all. "Have they taken any notice of you before?"

"Well, I believe they reviewed my application. They do that with all the new hires—even you. But I haven't had any direct dealings with them, no."

Small grunted. This was feeling more and more like a mug's game.

"Come on. Let's get some coffee and I'll tell you my game plan."

Maybe, Small thought, *this could qualify as an emergency, after all.*

CHAPTER THIRTEEN

Connor heard company coming well before they reached his loft. He quickly went down the hall and hid in a storage closet directly across from the stairs. He kept the door slightly ajar so he could get a look at who was visiting before they could get a look at him.

One person was coming up the stairs, quite close to the top floor. He heard another, more distant noise. Somebody else was using the stairs on the lower floors. The building had a few squatters besides Connor. They all made a practice of not bothering one another—sort of an unspoken code—usually keeping a floor or two between each apartment they had claimed. Connor was at the very top—the penthouse, Cordy had called it. She said it was the classiest place you could get, the penthouse. It didn't seem to matter to her that it was the penthouse of a dump.

The intruder on the stairs was definitely climbing all the way up, and was making no attempt to be quiet about it. The guys at Angel Investigations wouldn't be this noisy. Gunn and Wesley had a lot of practice stalking creatures of the night, and Angel, the man who was his physical, if not his spiritual, father—the *vampire* who was his father—was one of those creatures. Maybe some of those who worked with Holtz had found him. Holtz, the man whom he really thought of as his father, but a man who had died in such a way as to leave Connor doubting half of what he had learned in his childhood.

Connor wasn't sure at the best of times who was really on his side. Best, he thought, to hide and watch. He tensed his muscles, ready to attack.

He never expected Fred.

She walked straight past his hiding place, down the hall to knock on his door. "Connor? I need to talk to you."

Fred? Up here by herself? This wasn't exactly the safest corner of town, and while he was sure she had fought her share of demons, he couldn't see her showing up here without an armed escort. Something was wrong here. Was this some trick of Angel's after all?

He didn't sense anyone immediately behind her. There were still a couple of people moving around below, still making far less noise than what he'd just heard from Fred. But they didn't seem to be sneaking up on him. Probably just fellow squatters.

"Connor?" Fred shouted at the door. "I really need to talk to you. Please! It's dangerous for me to be here!"

She was alone, and she didn't appear to be holding any sort of weapon. He guessed it couldn't hurt to go out and talk to her.

He opened the closet door.

"Fred?"

She spun around with a gasp.

"Oh, Connor! Thank goodness you're here. I didn't know who else to turn to!"

For now, Connor kept his distance. "Who else? What do you mean? What about Gunn? What about Angel?"

Fred started to walk toward him. "They've all been taken! I only barely escaped. You're my only hope to save them!"

Save them? He wasn't sure he even wanted to do that. Still, Angel and his bunch had put down some pretty nasty demons and stuff since he'd gotten to know them. He could at least hear her out.

She hobbled a bit as she approached. Maybe that was why she had made so much noise on the stairs.

"I'm hurt, too. I think I've twisted my ankle. I was wondering if you could take a look at it." She pulled up her skirt so that he could take a better look at her leg.

"Connor!" another woman's voice shouted. "Stay away from that woman!"

He looked around. Cordy was coming up the stairs.

"Cordy! I wasn't . . . I mean I was just—"

Cordy waved him to come closer to her. "Don't worry. It's not your fault. She isn't who you think she is. Don't let her get too close to you."

Connor looked back and forth between the two women. They watched each other warily, as if each expected the other to attack at any second. "She isn't Fred?"

"She's a demon. A demon who's intent on destroying all of Angel's inner circle. And Connor, that includes you."

Cordy stepped between Connor and the thing he thought was Fred. Cordy had brought a large canvas bag with her. She fished inside it with her free hand and pulled out a machete.

She looked quite ready to use it. This was a side of Cordelia that Connor hadn't seen before.

"What are you trying to do?" Fred screeched. "I need help."

"You need to go back to whatever hellworld you came from. I know exactly what you are, and I'm not going to let you get Connor."

Fred waved her pale arms. "Connor! Don't

you see? She's gone crazy! She's the demon!"

Connor looked to Cordy. "I don't understand what's going on!"

"Oh, Connor! Save me!" Fred held out her arms in his direction. He had never seen her look so helpless.

Cordy nodded. "Well then, I guess I'd better show you." She ran toward Fred, the machete held away from her body.

Fred danced away from Cordy's swinging blade. She fell back against the wall, a movement that jarred her. For an instant, her human face melted, and Connor could see a jagged demon's face beneath.

The thing that wasn't Fred hissed at both of them.

"You can get rid of me for a little while," she called as she ducked another swing, "but we'll come back, over and over again, until we've destroyed you all."

"Why don't you just evaporate and leave us alone!" Cordy grabbed the machete with both hands and swung it again. It snagged and tore a bit of fabric from Fred's flowered dress.

Fred jumped in close to Cordy as soon as the blade passed. Connor saw a look of triumph in her eyes as she blew some strange, sparkling mist from her mouth. The mist glittered as it settled on Cordy's skin.

"We will take you next, Cordelia!" The smile on Fred's face turned to a look of confusion. "But you're . . . you don't have . . . how can—" She made choking noises, as though something was caught in her throat.

But Cordy had turned the machete around and swung it with all her strength. It cut deep into the flesh of Fred's hip.

The creature made a noise like stone grinding against stone.

"No! Your tricks mean nothing! We will take every one of you! We will defeat you!"

The thing that looked like Fred lost its shape, wavering first from flesh to stone then back to flesh again, then bursting like a plastic water bottle thrown down to the street.

Cordelia shook her head. "Demons." She smiled at Connor. "I'm glad you knew who to trust."

Connor smiled back. "I'll always trust you, Cordelia."

"I know. That's what makes our relationship so special."

Lorne came huffing and puffing up the stairs. "What's going on here? What did I miss?"

"Cordelia just killed a demon for me," Connor replied proudly.

"Well, unfortunately, the thing's not dead. I just sent it back home for a little while."

"Wow, our little miss here can put up quite a

pace." Lorne fluttered his hand admiringly at Cordelia as he paused to take a couple of deep breaths.

"Just thank me and my StairMaster," Cordy replied. She laid her hand gently on Connor's shoulders. "We need to get you out of here for a day or two. It's not safe to be by yourself."

"People are not who they seem," Lorne explained. "These demons can create near-perfect doubles of just about anybody."

"I think that thing tried to do something to Cordy," Connor replied. "But it didn't work."

Cordy shrugged. "I just got out of its way."

Connor thought it was more than that, but he supposed she was just being modest.

"Well," Lorne suggested, "let's get out of here before we have to fight anybody else."

Connor nodded. "I've got to grab a couple of things."

He'd let Cordelia explain the rest of what was happening on the way to the hotel.

Wesley always had such good intentions when he planned to meet Lilah. They would have a quiet conversation first, carefully doling out information—probably not everything, but enough so that both of them could get a better idea of what they were up against.

They had an understanding, after all. As much as

they had in common, they worked for opposite sides. They'd both be shocked if either one of them gave up too much.

But talking was important. Especially when they had a crisis on hand with a common enemy. They needed to get everything out in the open as quickly as possible.

He answered the door and invited her to come inside. Lilah was wearing a simple black dress. Not the sort of thing she would usually wear to the office, Wesley thought. It made her look stunning, as usual.

Their meeting also began as usual. He closed the door behind her. They exchanged the simplest of greetings. Neither one of them made any reference to earlier conversations.

Instead, they ended up pulling off each other's clothes. They were lucky this time, making it all the way to the bed.

They spent twenty minutes under the covers, their lovemaking ferocious, with a hint of the forbidden. At the end, they rolled apart on sweat-soaked sheets, both doing their best to catch their breath.

It was only after the physical part was over that they were able to talk.

Lilah regarded him in silence for a long moment before she initiated the conversation. "You probably shouldn't have let me in," she said in her usual wry tone. "I could have been one of them."

Wesley smiled back at that. "One has to live dangerously sometimes. Plus, it wasn't much of a risk. You've got the entire high-tech might of Wolfram and Hart behind you. I believe you're too well protected."

Lilah ran a perfectly manicured hand through her long brown hair as she considered his words. "When I'm physically within the confines of Wolfram and Hart, you're probably right. But even we have limited control over what goes on outside the firm. You of all people should know this."

Yes, Angel and associates had foiled the law firm's plans on numerous occasions. They'd even managed to invade Wolfram & Hart once or twice, despite all their security alarms and mystical protections. Wesley supposed other supernatural forces could have found their way into the law firm as well.

"And there's something I find even more worrying," Lilah continued. "These demons strike through individual personalities. Even the great Wolfram and Hart is only as strong as our weakest employee."

Wesley hadn't thought of that. "I suppose we actually have something of an advantage there. All of us at Angel Investigations know one another well—perhaps a bit too well."

"While we have hundreds of people associated

with our firm. The demons might find a way to infiltrate our ranks before we even notice." Lilah reached over and took his hand. "Believe it or not, I've been thinking seriously about this. We are both far too vulnerable to these demons. I'm thinking in this case we're on the same side."

"So we're together against the Seven Sinners."

"You've already determined who they are?" Lilah shook her head.

Wesley felt both surprised and a little proud that he had beaten the money-laden law firm to the punch. "Yes," he said with great humility, "just some simple research, the process of elimination. Of course, a number of my associates have had firsthand experience with the creatures."

"So much for the superiority of Wolfram and Hart technology. We had narrowed the potentials down to one of our three final choices. The Seven Sinners? They are the worst of the three. An extremely nasty bunch."

She rolled over on her back and stared at the ceiling for a moment. Wesley knew she was figuring how much she could safely pass on to him.

"It's the Sinners, then. One thing I *will* tell you. It is important for them to involve elements from both Angel's team and my law firm. For a true apocalypse, they need to engage both sides of the conflict."

"So we're both going to be involved in the

coming apocalypse?" Wesley had heard hints of this before, but this was the first time Lilah had addressed it directly.

"Both of us and everybody we know. And everybody we don't know. It makes sense, though. Everybody joins in when it's an apocalypse."

Her answer sounded more like the evasions and half-truths he was used to.

"So this is what all your computers and research tell you?" he prompted.

"The apocalypse?" Lilah shrugged. "With Angel as a major factor? It's very likely to happen. Sometimes predictions don't pan out. Sometimes they can be misinterpreted—"

Wesley bristled at that. "You know I know that all too well."

Lilah patted his shoulder reassuringly. "We all have our guilty secrets. And that is exactly what the members of the Remorse wish to target."

Wesley realized she was right. Everyone has their regrets. He might never live down his misstep with Angel's son, Connor. Gunn carried a similar burden. His sister had been attacked and killed on his watch. Angel had centuries of bloodletting that he still sometimes struggled to come to terms with. Everyone associated with Angel—probably even Lilah—had his or her regrets.

"And you?" he asked.

"Regrets?" she said with a sad smile. "When you

do what I do, you put them away in a little box on the side, but they never go away. But then you don't open the box either."

"But about this apocalypse," he prompted. The more they knew about the demon's plans, the more effective they might be in panning counter-measures.

"What can I say? While I'm not at liberty to give you the details, it's big. Apparently the Sinners want as many of us as possible to be involved. But their apocalypse will take on quite a different form."

"Different?"

"All they really want for now is the energy of the initial conflict. Once they get that working, they set their own end-of-the-world in motion."

"You've obviously gotten more information on these demons than I have."

"Our database includes information collected through a number of different dimensions. Some of them have seen the Sinners before. A few worlds have even survived their onslaught. These crea-tures live to build up a conflict, then tear a hole in the middle of it." She frowned. "And then, once they have subverted our destiny, they'll feed off the guilt of the world."

Wesley's reading was starting to make sense. "So that's what it means—the Great Remorse. Everyone reliving their guilt while the demons feed on their emotions?"

"I think you get the picture."

He sighed, and moved closer to Lilah. "We're all guilty, aren't we?" He looked deep into Lilah's eyes. "Though some of us are more guilty than others."

Lilah stretched and smiled. She let the sheet fall off her naked form. "Tell me what a bad girl I've been."

They both sat up as they heard the sound of breaking glass.

"The window in the kitchen, I think," Wesley said. "Apparently, we're not alone."

Lilah rolled quickly out of bed, pulling her black dress back over her head. "Well, let's deal with them."

Wesley jumped out the other side and pulled on his pants. "I could probably get help here in less than five minutes."

Lilah reached for her purse. "I could get somebody here in two."

Wesley heard a second crash, followed by a loud thump. "I don't think we have two minutes," he replied. "Have you got your gun?"

Lilah pulled a slim, silver revolver from her bag. "Never without it."

"Good. I think we can stop these things if we attack from a distance." Wesley pulled his own gun out of the nightstand drawer. More traditional weapons were often the best for handling supernatural creatures, who could only be killed by a stake through the heart or severing the head from the body. This was an entirely different brand of beast. If these demons wanted to mimic humans so badly, they could be stopped with good old American bullets.

They stepped out of the bedroom, Wesley first, Lilah close behind. She took the left-hand side of the living room while he walked around the couch on the right, each systematically checking their surroundings for hidden intruders as they moved to the kitchen.

Wesley caught movement through the kitchen door. These demons were persistent, but they weren't subtle. A man was pulling a woman into the kitchen through the broken window. They were making quite a lot of noise in doing so. Wesley didn't recognize either one of the newcomers. "Do you know either of these people?" he whispered.

Lilah shook her head.

A sudden doubt struck Wesley. "What if they're human?"

"What are the chances of that?" Lilah said skeptically. She lifted her gun and took aim. "So we just wing them. Maybe we can keep them alive long enough to ask a question or two."

Wesley thought of the cell phone in his jacket pocket. "I still wish I had time to bring in my crew. I probably shouldn't have gone off alone."

"You're not alone."

The woman pulled free of the window and swung herself over the countertop to land on the kitchen floor. The intruders looked directly at Lilah and Wesley.

The man reached inside his leather jacket. He had a gun of his own.

Wesley fired off a single round.

The man spun around as he took a bullet in the shoulder. His face shifted from flesh to rock and back again. The woman jumped out of the way.

"Definitely demons," Lilah agreed.

The man was writhing in agony on the floor. The woman was out of sight, hiding behind the cabinets.

"Just another quiet night at home," Wesley said as they stepped forward into the kitchen. "This might have been a bit more than you bargained for."

Lilah smiled back at him. "Nonsense. This is my favorite part of the job." She moved to his side. "See how easy it is to work together?"

He waved for her to step clear of the counters. He needed a clear line of fire for the other demon. "Nothing we do is ever easy."

Lilah trained her gun on the demon writhing on the floor. "Well, you certainly don't have to tell Angel about this. It could be just another one of our little secrets."

Wesley didn't reply. He couldn't have any more secrets. It was holding information in, and keeping his own fears too close to his chest, that had almost gotten himself killed, had almost destroyed all of them. "We'll have to talk about this later."

He slowly swept his gun back and forth as he walked across the kitchen. The area in front of the appliances was clear. Apparently no demons had entered before the two they had seen. What you see is what you get.

The woman rushed out from her hiding place. Wesley spun, following her movement and firing off three quick shots. One of the rounds caught the creature full in the chest.

She screamed, her form losing shape, from flesh to rock to a flash of liquid.

"So much for winging them," Lilah said wryly.

Wesley looked down at the rapidly disappearing puddle on the floor. "So long as we're safe."

Lilah waved her gun at the male demon lying still on the kitchen floor. "Since this one still looks human, that means he's still functioning. Handy that they do that for us." She kicked his leg with her toe. "Maybe we can get him to talk."

With a sudden roar, the man rose from the ground and launched himself toward Lilah.

Wesley stepped in the way of the demon's charge, his gun at the ready.

The demon released its crystalline mist as Wesley

shot it between the eyes. The mists settled around Wesley. The demon fell apart, just like its female counterpart.

Wesley took a deep breath. "I guess he didn't want to talk."

Lilah looked down at what was left of her attacker. She ran her free hand through her hair. "That was quite gallant of you, you know." She looked back at Wesley. "Probably has something to do with your being British."

"No doubt," Wesley replied. He was surprisingly shaken by what had just happened.

"But Wesley, dear," Lilah said with a frown, "I'm afraid you've been compromised."

Wesley brushed at the skin on his arms. His flesh felt as though he had been sprayed with cold cooking oil.

Lilah waved at the fading glitter. "We can remove this. We've set up a decontamination room for this very purpose. We can remove this demon mark from everybody who's been affected."

"If it means we have to come into Wolfram and Hart? I don't believe my compatriots will be too keen on that idea."

"You can come in now, alone, for a start. No one else has to know."

He thought again about having too many secrets.

"Once you've been cleaned off, we can tell the others. It's the best way for us to defeat those things."

She was probably right. But there was something else he had to do first. "In the meantime, though, they've just managed to manufacture a demon version of me. It takes a while for them to be created, and then to leave their nest. From what I've seen before, I would guess we have an hour."

"We should do this sooner than later," Lilah replied. "The doubles slowly bleed energy from the originals, from what I understand. It becomes quite noticeable in a day or two."

Wesley thought about Fred's complaints of being tired. "If I can't do in my double in a matter of hours, I'll come in. I'll do my best to get Fred and Gunn to come in as well."

"That would certainly help to stem the tide. One of our operatives has been compromised. He's a new hire, but he works under me."

"So you're involved in the apocalypse?"

"Apparently the demons think so. Wolfram and Hart has been through a number of botched apocalypses. Some, we even helped to bring about. We do have a history before you folks came to town, you know. But not with these creatures." She sighed. "I'll have my subordinate go through the decontamination first, to prove to you it's safe."

"It sounds like you're not sure it's safe either."

"It's a new procedure, based on old manuscripts. There's always an uncertainty factor."

"And this new hire is expendable?"

"Certainly more expendable than you are."

"Well, I think that's the nicest thing you've said to me in quite some time."

"Don't let it go to your head. You have my number. Call me before it gets too late."

"I need to call Angel first."

Lilah shrugged. She knew the pecking order. "Do what you have to do. But I don't want to lose any more in this fight than we have to."

Wesley raised his eyebrows in surprise. "Now it's you who's sounding gallant."

"Hey, I just want to survive. The only way we're going to come out of this intact is by working together."

"All right. Let me make plans with Angel. I'll call you later."

Lilah walked back toward the bedroom to fetch the rest of her clothes. "Hey! Where have I heard that one before?"

CHAPTER FOURTEEN

Grady Small had far too much time to think.

They had found him a place to sleep, a nice place, too, on one of the upper floors of the office building. Some kind of "special guest quarters," as David described it. It was a small apartment, really. Three rooms, including a fully stocked bar and refrigerator. After David left, he cased the place and discovered it didn't have any windows, either. The curtains covered nothing but bare walls.

How did he end up here? In Small's current condition, David didn't think the ex-cop should be outside of Wolfram & Hart's supervision. He had enough seniority to authorize the room. Small should just sit back and enjoy it. In the morning, David would return and tell Small his part in the master plan.

"Current condition?" Small fully knew it was David who was keeping him from getting rid of the demon's mark. David wanted to keep him quiet until he could use him.

He looked at the bar, fully stocked with name brands and more—there was a nice bottle of twelve-year-old scotch right up front—along with a few bottles of vintage wine and champagne. He opened the doors to the refrigerator. The freezer was full of salmon, shrimp, and steak, as well as a few simpler things with instructions for preparation in the microwave. The refrigerator below contained fresh fruit and prepared salads, along with soda and imported water and beer. He hadn't eaten this well in many restaurants.

After a moment's thought, he pulled out a prepared meal from above, something Mexican, and then grabbed a Dos Equis beer from the fridge. He slid the frozen meal into the microwave and uncapped the bottle with an opener that he found in the first drawer. He wasn't really very hungry. Somehow, it all seemed like he was fixing a last meal for the condemned.

It was funny how all the bits of his life felt like they had come together, only to go crazy, out of his control. In his forty-plus years of living, he had never particularly been a big-picture kind of guy, always grabbing for the quick reward rather than the long-term goal. He had scraped through college, had had a run of failed relationships, then finally had gotten kicked off the force. Despite all his screw-ups, he had thought he had landed on his feet, but it looked like everything around him was nothing but quicksand.

They had given him a few hours to sleep. David said he had big plans, but that they were better followed during the daylight hours. Unlike vampires, these demons could be on your case twenty-four hours a day. Small did not find this fact the least bit reassuring.

He had tried to persuade David to do things differently. Get Small protected, bring in Lilah Morgan and some of the big guns.

His keeper had tried at first to make a joke out of his objections. When Small persisted, David's remarks had turned to not-so-veiled threats.

"You don't want a bad evaluation. Trust me. Especially when you have no track record, no seniority. We have a lot of *special* projects here at Wolfram and Hart. You'll be volunteered. By me, of course. But since you won't survive the experience, who will know?"

He imagined Lilah Morgan could put a stop to all of this. If he could only get in touch with her. He wished, when he had called her before, he had thought to leave a message. She'd probably be tracking him down by now.

Unless David was working under *her* orders. Anything was possible in a place like this.

He didn't see a phone in this apartment. Stereo,

large-screen TV, a bed twice the size of something you'd find in a hotel. The first thing he'd done after David left was to try the door, which had locked as soon as David had pulled it shut behind him. Plenty of ways to kill time, but no way to get out of there.

He pulled his cell phone from his pocket. He wondered if he could still get a signal going out. The way they had him locked up tight, the walls in there could be lined with lead.

It was worth a try.

He checked his watch. It was close to 2 A.M. If Ms. Morgan wasn't answering her phone three hours ago, she certainly wouldn't be now. Oh well, he could still leave a message. If David didn't set his plans in motion too early in the morning, it might still do Small some good.

He punched in the boss's number.

"Lilah Morgan." She answered on the second ring.

"Uh," Small replied. He never expected to have her answer the phone. "Grady Small here. I didn't expect—"

"This is my private line. I'm almost always available here. I imagine you have something important to report."

"Uh, yes. I don't know how to put this."

"As simply as possible. I've already had a long night. Have they put you through the decontamination process?"

He told her why David didn't think that was such a good idea.

"I see." Her voice betrayed no emotion, staying as businesslike as before. "So that means David has further plans?"

Small explained how David had set up a meeting with the enemy in the morning, with Small serving as bait.

"Thank you again for keeping me informed. I think I want to provide some input into David's plans. When this is all over, I'll see you get some reward."

"Should I do anything?"

"Just proceed with David's directions. There will be some changes, but they will not be implemented by David. Thank you for keeping me informed."

She cut the connection.

Whew. Small guessed he'd gotten what he wanted. But the coolness of Ms. Morgan's tone had been unsettling.

It sounded like tomorrow would see a change of plans. Maybe Small had saved his bacon by destroying David's career. Well, the guy deserved it. He'd see what happened when you threatened Grady Small.

He snapped his phone closed and put it back in his pocket. He was learning to work the system here, just like he had done in his days back on the force. And the first part of working the system was to stay on Lilah Morgan's good side.

Now he was actually a little hungry. He ate some of the burrito he'd heated in the microwave. It was every bit as tasty as he'd imagined. He finished off his beer and decided he could use a couple hours of sleep.

"Mr. Small."

The voice kept repeating the same two words. Very insistent. Very close to his ear.

"Mr. Small. It's time for you to get up."

Small opened his eyes, half-expecting someone to be standing over him. But he saw no one in the room.

"Mr. Marsh has informed me that he will be arriving in one half hour. Please be ready."

It was a speaker, hidden in the headboard. God knew what else they had planted in here. Hidden cameras, probably.

He wondered if Mr. Marsh and Ms. Morgan had spoken. Or maybe David had watched and recorded everything he had said to their boss before Lilah could make contact.

She had told him to go ahead with the meet. As little as that appealed to him, he knew it was his best chance for survival.

He had laid out the situation last night. There was nothing else that he could add. There wasn't anything he could say that would change her mind.

She had talked about a reward. He wondered if it would be waiting for him in heaven.

He climbed out of bed and discovered that his suit was no longer draped across the couch where he had left it the night before. Instead, it was hung neatly just inside the front door. He walked across the room to take a closer look. His suit, along with his shirt and tie, had been cleaned and pressed while he slept. His shoes had been polished. A bag with underwear and socks, not just the correct size, but the brands he usually chose, hung over the hanger as well.

His cell phone was no longer in his pocket. It wasn't in the underwear bag or set aside anyplace that he could see. He guessed that David had been listening in, and had decided to let him know who was boss.

So it came to this. David was in control. And Grady Small would be killed in some fool plan concocted by a corporate wiseass.

At least they had let him keep his gun. It hung in its holster just the way he'd left it, fully loaded. It made sense, he supposed. Shooting his superior wouldn't do him any good at all. He guessed, in this case, the phone was the more dangerous weapon.

He put on some gourmet coffee while he took a quick shower. If it was his last day on earth, at least he was going to look presentable.

The bell rung as he was knotting his tie. The

door popped open without Small taking a step toward it.

David Marsh was all smiles. "Have a good rest?"

"I've had better." He decided it was time to be direct. "What did you do with my cell phone?"

David looked confused. "Pardon? I left orders to have your suit cleaned. Was the phone with it? It must have been misplaced. An oversight, I'm sure."

Small stared back at his superior. If that was the way they were going to play it, he didn't have anything to say.

"Grady, Grady, Grady," David insisted. "We have to be on the same page here."

Small sighed. He guessed he was in this until he could find a way out. "I'll do what you need me to do. But I haven't had much input here."

"You won't need to do much at all. I've thought of everything. These demons want you so badly, they're going to stroll right into our trap."

Small frowned. "How can you trap them? Won't they just evaporate the way they usually do?"

David was smiling enough for both of them. "We have ways of neutralizing the shapeshifting, keeping them in one form. I've had a van rigged specially. It will pick them right off the street. We'll have them cut off from their source of power, get a real chance to examine them."

He paused to look at Small, the smile fading on his face. "I know you don't like me. And you probably don't think much of my plan. Work with me here. You have to have some talent to get as far as I have in this firm. And I intend to go farther. Once this job is done, I'll see you'll get something extra for your cooperation."

So he'd been offered something extra, from both Marsh and Morgan? Apparently, Grady Small would get rewarded however things turned out. It was a sweet deal, if he was still alive.

David checked his watch. "We've got half an hour before we meet our demons. Just enough time to get our team in order. Shall we go?"

Small let David lead the way.

They took the elevator down together. It opened on the firm's main lobby.

Everyone smiled pleasantly and said hello as they passed, as if this was your typical working day. Small felt like a character in a play, acting like everything was perfectly normal, when they were actually looking at the end of the world.

Maybe the end of the world was business as usual around here.

They stepped outside.

It was a bright, cheery morning. Typical L.A. weather. Just another perfect day before the apocalypse.

"We're meeting them behind the building,"

David explained. "It's just a couple of blocks. We'll go on foot."

Small fell into step at David's side. He glanced around as casually as possible, both to see if they were being followed and to search for possible routes of escape, just in case this fellow's plan didn't go off quite as scheduled.

He felt better simply being free of that building. What else could he do?

Small decided he'd at least enjoy the sunlight one final time.

CHAPTER FIFTEEN

The Seven, together, could not be defeated.

This world was so rich, so full of the road not taken, so ripe with what might have been. Anger and fear were everywhere. Harsh words, raised voices, misunderstandings that lasted generations, differences that led to clenched fists, or blades or guns or bombs. And it all left a trail of what the Seven needed most: the glory of guilt, the mother who rejects the child, the child who rebels against the mother, the father who leaves the family, the spouses who harbor secret longings they can never share, tearing their unions apart. The harsh word at the wrong time, the accident after too much partying, the gun in hand at the imperfect moment. These humans lived millions of these events, sometimes mere seconds in duration. Ah, but they nurtured these moments of misery, and honed them to accompany them through a lifetime.

It was such an opulent vein of despair, and the Seven would gorge themselves upon it.

They were strongest when united—and in their original form, before they put on their masks of flesh. They could plan then, when they were one, above the petty concerns of their duplicated hosts.

One mortal after another, the Seven first copied their forms and then stole their energy. The Lords of the Remorse could feel the strength grow within them.

The Seven could overcome any obstacle. Phil Manchester discovered their existence before their plans were fully formed. He tried to subvert their goals, but he led them right to their final destiny.

Yet he had given his notes to the other detectives. Manchester's notes had robbed the Sinners of the element of surprise. The Seven had tried to retrieve the document, only to reveal themselves more fully to those who must succumb.

The Seven had joined again after that, and chosen a more frontal assault, moving quickly forward, contaminating their prey even if it meant being shattered and sent back to the Stone. While each setback diminished them, every new death gave them more than enough strength to compensate.

But the Seven needed something more—a crisis worthy of their attention, a drama so big, it might dwarf all the petty problems of the world and change the whole of existence upon this plane.

They had found it here, in a city called Los Angeles, centered on a creature called Angel and all those around him.

They took on one human form after another to learn how this world functioned, so they might best tear it apart to suit their needs. Their individual parts stumbled, and even succumbed to near-human weakness. Only when they joined again could they be fully as one in their quest for the goal.

They needed one strong enough, to carry this plan forward as they spent time in their weaker, separate forms. But the Remorse would provide. The center of the crisis was exactly what they needed.

Their copies found the worst aspects of their prey to build upon, the dark side of every one of their victims. But Angel had a dark side that made even the Sinners take notice. Angelus had a history bathed in blood.

Angelus was strong enough to end the world, and Angel's guilt would fuel the apocalypse.

Once they had recruited him, their individual personalities would fall into line. Differences would be forgotten.

Armageddon would be theirs. And they would drink the guilt of a billion souls.

Wondrous would be the Remorse. This world would suffer so. And then, when it was drained and lifeless at last, the Seven Sinners would take another world, and another.

It was a most satisfying existence.

At last, Angel thought, they had everybody together, sitting around the lobby of the Hyperion Hotel. At least everyone was physically present. Wesley looked a little the worse for wear, probably from his recent tussle with the demon. Fred and Gunn sat next to each other, but didn't touch, as if neither of them felt like they were quite themselves. Connor crouched on his haunches in a corner, just beyond Cordy. He looked angry and ready to bolt at any excuse. Lorne was the only one who looked the least bit relaxed. But then, he had just gotten everybody to sing again. Besides some minor evidence of Wesley's encounter with the demon, everything was, Lorne's exact word, "A-OK."

Just their one big happy family, together again. The singing had done nothing to cheer people up. If anything, they seem to have gotten more depressed.

"What?" Cordy asked the crowd. "People don't like *The Sound of Music*?"

"This still isn't going our way," Angel began. "The demons seem to know just where we're going to be. Well, they do have our memories, at least a lot of them. But we seem to be scrambling just to keep up. And they seem ready to trap us every time any one of us goes off alone." He looked pointedly at Wesley, who nodded glumly.

Angel clapped his hands. "So no more being alone. From now on, we act together—as one mean fighting machine." He surveyed the whole gang. "Any suggestions on how to start?"

"First we have to determine their weaknesses," Wesley said. "We have to strike at their most vulnerable point."

"The Stone," Fred piped up. She gripped Phil's notes in her hands. "That's what Phil said they seemed the most afraid of—when he tried to grab the Stone."

"Sounds like a plan," Angel agreed. "Gunn, you and I are going back to that warehouse. We're taking that stone into custody."

"That could be quite interesting," Wesley agreed. "According to my research, the demons must return to the Stone to regenerate. I suppose that's why they don't really die—the seven doubles are simply projections, powered by the Stone."

"Even more reason to get that rock," Gunn added.

"Should we be able to get all seven of them into the stone at the same time," Wesley mused, "maybe we could put an end to this for good.

"In the meantime, though, the demons are going to keep busy trying to kill their doubles.

Especially the doubles that came before us. According to the information I received from Lilah, we are their ultimate goal—the last humans they copy before the apocalypse."

"Lilah?" Gunn bristled. "If you trust her—"

"In this instance, she is in as much danger as we are. Our goals, at least for the moment, are the same as Wolfram and Hart's."

"But can we save any of the others?" Fred waved the notes. "The ones that came before us, like Phil, and the ones on Phil's list."

Wesley paused for a moment before he replied. "At most, only a couple of those on the list would still be around. Most of the people named there have been taken over by doubles of us—Fred, Gunn, and me. Then we know of Phil. I understand that one of Wolfram and Hart's operatives, a Grady Small, was also infected. Perhaps Phil could tell us if we have any hope of contacting the ones who remain."

Fred nodded. "I'll give him a call."

Gunn stood and looked toward the door. "After they kill whoever else is out there, they'll be coming after us. For the final showdown."

Angel didn't want that showdown to start any faster than was absolutely necessary. He had doubts about talking to anybody over the phone who had been doubled. He turned back to Fred. "It would probably be better if, say, you and Cordy could go there in person, see that Phil's still bandaged and in his bed." Angel saw the look his son gave him. "Connor could go too. If we stay together, the demons won't surprise us."

Wesley nodded. "I'll try to find a way to impede the Seven's progress."

"I wonder if Phil is well enough to leave the hospital," Fred added. "We could put him up here. If what you say is true, they'll redouble their efforts to kill him, too."

"I've got a question," Connor piped up. "Is there anybody these demons couldn't copy? And then can't kill?"

Wesley frowned, tapping the book before him. "It might certainly be possible. I imagine it would hamper their movement greatly."

"Cordy found a way around them," Connor said with a proud grin. "It was awesome!"

But Cordelia shook her head. "It was just dumb luck. I think I stopped it before it could play the name game with my soul." She looked a bit embarrassed, as though she didn't want to be singled out.

"Hey," Angel said softly. "You did good work."

She shrugged. "Probably all that time I can't remember up there with the higher powers."

"Maybe if you have no memories," Gunn suggested, "they can't really grab on to you."

No one added anything else. They had an actual moment of silence. Angel realized, since all of this had begun, that there had been hardly any bickering. Everyone had a job to do. They were always best in times of crisis.

"Lorne and Wesley will watch the hotel," Angel concluded. "Any more questions?"

Nobody spoke. They were ready for action.

Angel smiled, ever so slightly. "Then let's get these demons where they hurt."

Phil had to get out of there.

He was finally feeling more like his old self—if a little dragged out. Ever since he'd had the run-in with the demons, it was like he had a flu he couldn't quite shake. But the wound was healing fine. He managed to climb out of bed. And just in bloody time.

The cops had been pulled off their detail, just like that. One of them said the orders came from upstairs. He mentioned a couple of names Phil knew from some of the stranger cases he had been involved in, influential people who worked on the edges of society. In short, this all had something to do with Wolfram & Hart.

He walked to the door, cracked it open, and listened. Nobody was around. Even the nurses' station was deserted.

He slowly dressed in his ragged and torn street clothes, careful of his bandages.

He heard a rap on the door.

"Yes?" he called out cautiously. He looked around for something he could use to defend himself.

Winifred Burkle stuck her head in the door. "Hi, Phil!"

Phil paused in his search for a weapon. "Fred? Is it really you?"

"I know. You can't trust anybody these days." She pushed the door open the rest of the way. "I brought Cordy. I figured if there was more than one of us, you'd know it was really us."

"And who's this?" Phil asked when he saw a gangly teenager hovering behind the two women.

"You haven't met Connor?" Cordy asked. "Let's just say he's a friend of the family."

"Phil, something's going on in this hospital," Fred continued. "We walked right in here. There doesn't seem to be a doctor or nurse on the entire floor, and we didn't see any security on the way up."

Phil told them what he had overheard.

"Wolfram and Hart?" Fred replied with a frown. "That doesn't sound right. Unless Wesley was wrong about them being threatened as well."

She shook her head. "But we've come to get you out of here. We figure things are going to start happening even faster around here. Angel and Gunn have gone after the Stone."

. "At the warehouse? Who knows if it's still there." Phil realized there were so many things he hadn't had a chance to tell them. "They move it around a lot. In the end, you know, they'll bring the Stone to you."

Connor spun around. "There's somebody else here!"

A thin man in a trench coat ducked into another one of the patient rooms. It was the other Phil. The real Phil shivered as though someone had just walked over his grave.

"I'll catch him," Connor announced.

The nursing unit was a big rectangle in the center of the floor. The other Phil had disappeared in a doorway halfway down the hall. Connor circled around the station so he could look through the doorway from a distance

"Connor!" Cordy called. "Watch out."

"Hey," Connor replied with a grin, "I was raised to not trust anybody." He crept across the nurses' station, to reach the far side of the door.

Fred yawned. She shook her head. "I can't seem to stay awake."

"It's the demons," a cultured voice said from the far end of the hall. "They drain your energy once they've touched your soul. You've got to kill them before they kill you."

"Wesley?" Fred said. "Shouldn't you be back at the hotel?"

"Watch out!" Couldn't they see? Phil stepped in front of the women. "That isn't Wesley!"

"He's gone!" Connor called, appearing at the end of the hallway. "There was another door in the room."

"Ah, the very lad I'm looking for." Wesley turned to Connor. A crystalline mist shot from his mouth.

"Looking for me?" The other Phil stepped out from behind the nurses' station and shot the real item three times in the chest.

This was going down.

They had gone out in Angel's car as soon as the sun went down. Angel drove them straight to the warehouse where he'd found the demons the night before.

Gunn had to shake himself awake. Fred had complained about being down. It was starting to get him, too.

Gunn let Angel lead the way into the old warehouse. The dump looked abandoned, like it hadn't been used for legit business in years. He was sure the joint had seen its share of drug deals and homeless squatters before the demons moved in. Now the lowlifes would probably be as far away as possible. When something strange goes down, word moves fast on the street.

"Careful," warned Angel. "There's all kinds of garbage thrown around in here."

Enough moonlight filtered through the broken windows along the hall to show that Angel spoke

true. Rags, boxes, fast-food cartons, broken liquor
bottles. You name it, it was someplace in this hallway.

"Watch out for the hole." Angel and Gunn both
skirted a pit in the middle of the floor.

"It's awfully quiet here," Gunn whispered.

"It was quiet here last time, at least until I got to
the big storeroom. I think these guys specialize in
ambushes."

They crept carefully down the hall, listening for
any sound of company. If anything, the trash was
piled higher the farther they walked.

Gunn kicked a moldy cardboard box out of their
way. "I guess they don't want the Good
Housekeeping Seal of Approval?"

"World-destroying demons probably aren't big on
domestic skills." They had reached a cross-corridor.
Angel looked up and down the length of the halls,
then waved for Gunn to follow. "They had the Stone
right through here."

Gunn braced himself as they entered the room.
It was empty. "There's nobody around."

"The Stone should be right over . . . it's not
there."

"Maybe they got a hiding place."

Angel surveyed the room. "It's a big rock, maybe
half the size of you or me. It wouldn't be that easy
to hide. Maybe they threw a tarp over it, or it's in
one of these old crates."

Gunn walked slowly across the cracked concrete floor. "At least it's not as dirty in here as it is out front."

"Yeah, I noticed that too. It was cleaner in here earlier, too, but it wasn't this clean. It's like they've taken all the important junk out of here."

"So they're gone? And they took the Stone?"

"Looks that way. But where would they have taken it?"

"Someplace else they could hide. This isn't the only empty warehouse."

Gunn had a horrible thought. "Or someplace they were planning to use it."

"You mean, while we came out here—"

"They took the Stone to the hotel. It makes sense. The only advantage we had was whenever we stopped those things, they had to pop back out of the Stone and then get halfway across the town.

"They've got to get it to the center of the action," Gunn continued. "If the crystal's right there, they can go after us, over and over again."

"We've got to get back." Angel turned to hurry back to the car,

"I'll call ahead on my cell."

Angel looked confused for a moment. "Oh, your phone. Your cell phone." He shook his head. "I knew we were staying in pairs for a reason."

CHAPTER SIXTEEN

The demon Grady was free of the others again. The Sinners were so smug. Thought they were better than somebody with the resources of the new, improved Grady Small. Seven Different Pieces of the Great Remorse, each one worthless without the rest. He supposed he believed it, too, at least a little, when he was joined with the others. But it was only when he broke away that he felt truly free.

The Remorse had no need for this Angelus. He would show them who their true leader was.

Only he could get into Wolfram & Hart. Only he could make the apocalypse whole. And now he would kill his other self, and get a taste of real power.

He had convinced some of the others to join him. He brought the new Phil and Gunn and Fred. He thought some familiar faces might add to the confusion.

And, of course, there was David Marsh. These corporate types were so easy to dupe. They were so caught up in their own lies that they couldn't see the greater lies that were going to swallow them whole.

Soon, the balance would be struck, and the Remorse would begin.

Lilah Morgan stood in the security office, watching her soon to be dismissed assistant walk across the plaza in front of Wolfram & Hart.

He knew nothing about the true chain of command.

She had already informed the higher-ups. David's surprise might be ruined, but the Seven Sinners would be taught a lesson they would not forget.

The security people David had enlisted had already informed her of their instructions, how they had been directed to trap the demons and at least neutralize one of them in the van. She had her own people monitoring the action as well, ready to move in on her orders.

The plan had a fair probability of success. It was a shame that David hadn't gone through proper channels. Now, once he had gained his prize, she would simply confiscate it in the name of the senior partners. And, poor, poor David?

She would have to post the opening of the

assistant's position to human resources by the end of the day.

Grady Small was operating on automatic pilot. He was reminded of his days as a rookie cop, when he and his partner had been pinned down in a cross fire between warring factions from some drug deal gone bad. Bullets were flying everywhere. It felt like suddenly the whole world was crashing down on him.

"Keep your head down, kid. You'll be fine."

He had spent his entire career keeping his head down. Until now, when it was going to be served up on a silver platter. Not that there couldn't be some way out of this. Back in the day, caught in the cross fire, he would have used his partner for a shield. Today, he would sacrifice David Marsh in a heartbeat.

The two men walked across the plaza side by side. Small knew they weren't facing the enemy alone. It didn't make him feel any better. His ass was on the firing line.

David had recruited two young, heavyset men who were apparently incapable of smiling. They did say, "Certainly, Mr. Marsh," a number of times. It was probably the first time Grady Small had heard somebody use David's last name as a term of respect.

"They're both expert marksmen," David explained.

"They'll flank us." David briefly instructed the gunmen in a voice so soft that Small could only make out the occasional word:

"Shoot . . . signal . . . out of the van . . . arm or leg . . . we'll close in on them . . . last resort."

The marksmen faded back into the crowd.

David offered Small his winning smile. "They're good men. Everything will go according to plan. Let's go. We've got an appointment to keep."

They walked in silence until they reached the street, passing the loading docks and the back entrance to the underground garage.

"Things are going to start happening right around this corner," David said cheerily. "Don't worry, we won't let them get too close."

Small was suddenly aware of his own gun, bumping against his rib cage in the shoulder holster. "Who do we shoot?"

"Anybody who threatens us. It's just important to keep one of them alive."

"So you can deliver him personally to the senior partners?"

"Exactly. Grady Small, we are looking at a very bright future indeed." David flipped his cell phone open. "Excuse me. I need to get things in motion."

"There's nothing else you want to tell me?"

"Just follow my lead," David replied. "It's as easy as pie."

• • •

Lilah knew it was time for action.

David had made a pair of calls. The first was to get the van in position. The second was to an unknown party, only to say two words: "We're on." That meant he had another confederate or two that Lilah didn't know about yet.

David was the sort to always have a few backup plans.

He was meeting the demons just beyond the perimeter of the normal range of the Wolfram & Hart surveillance cameras. The meet would take place across the street from their headquarters, just outside the entranceway to an office building site still under construction. She supposed David wanted to make the grab off-site so it could be a bigger surprise when he brought one of the creatures in. It did show a certain flair for the dramatic.

She managed to have security reposition one of the cameras to give her a partial view of the meeting place. She saw three people waiting there: Winifred Burkle, Charles Gunn, and Phil Manchester. She knew they only looked like those people. They were most certainly their demon doubles. It was a rather large group for David and Grady Small to confront and overwhelm. And, speaking of Grady, where was his double?

This was looking more problematic than Lilah had first anticipated. She looked to the head of security.

"We may need more backup on this. Can you get a few more men to the back of the plaza?"

The security chief looked to a large personnel grid that monitored the whereabouts of all his guards. "I could have two good men back there in about two minutes. Half a dozen more would take another five."

"Two good men it will have to be. Have them hang back at first, but be ready for my signal. And make sure they're armed." She turned to head for the garage. "Oh, and call upstairs. I'll be in touch."

She had arranged for a car and driver so that she, too, could be at the rendezvous point in less than a minute. The elevator was waiting. Lilah rested her hand on her handgun.

Poor David. Bringing the demons right to their door, and he wouldn't even be here tomorrow. All that talent gone to waste.

She might even get a promotion out of this.

This was goin' down.

The other Gunn, the better Gunn, waited with Fred and Phil in the shade by the new office place. They were supposed to be the bait. But he didn't think those jerks at Wolfram & Hart had ever seen bait this lively.

"Keep to the shadows. Don't make yourself an easy target. Jump when I tell you to go." That's

what they told them, and this time, Gunn was
willing. The Seven Sinners were about to get
themselves a couple of new recruits. He gave
Fred a little squeeze for luck, and she squeezed
him back, hard. That wild child was probably
ready to do the deed right here, right now. Too
bad they had different priorities just this moment.
Still, he had just enough time to turn around,
bend down, and plant a deep, deep kiss.

"Heads up, kiddies," Phil said. "We've got
company."

It was the van. They'd been told to expect the
van. It had dark black windows so you couldn't see
inside. The van pulled to the curb and stopped in
front of the entrance with its motor running.

Here came more company too: David, and
Grady Small—the human Grady Small—walking
past the loading dock, then beyond the ramp down
to the garage.

Both of them turned as the garage door rumbled
open. They looked like they were surprised. Gunn
didn't think this was part of their plan. He thought
his Grady Small, the better Grady Small, was hiding in one of the low windows of the empty building behind him.

It looked like they had an extra player or two.
The car was pretty much a match for the van, a
sleek black sedan solid as a tank, with windows
every bit as dark.

The car pulled behind the van and waited, engine running.

"That car?" David called ahead. "That car's nothing. The money's inside the van."

Money? Oh yeah, that was the cover story. Somebody was screwin' with them. Gunn wasn't sure who. The plan had sounded neat and quick. Now it was lookin' messy around the edges.

David waved for Small to follow him across the street. They jogged around the back of the mystery car.

Grady Small was almost to the sweet spot. David moved away from him.

The car door opened right after they passed.

But who was comin' out of the car? Lilah Morgan? This wasn't part of any plan he'd heard of.

Who cares? She was too late to do anything. Gunn would give it ten seconds before all hell broke loose. He smiled at that. Looked like the girlie was in for a surprise.

Maybe, Grady Small thought, he should just run the hell away from here. David would probably hire someone to track him down, but hey, he'd live another day or two.

He heard the gunshot a second after the bullet hit his right shoulder, spinning him around.

Small swore. They had a sniper. Was this part of the great David's plan? He let his momentum take him down to the ground and he landed on his back, on his good shoulder. It still hurt like hell. But he'd be less of a target close to the ground like this.

Somebody got out of the car. He heard other doors open, too, saw Lilah Morgan and the driver walk around the sedan, guns raised. Two other men—the men David had talked to before—stepped out of the van. So this was how Lilah was going to handle it. She had her own gun at the ready, and was shouting orders to people across the street.

But it wasn't enough to cover the three of them out in the open. They had to get the sniper, or he could pick them off one by one. His rescuers would end up just as dead as Small.

Another shot got one of the guys from the van. The force of the bullet threw the man back into the street. It was a clean kill, right through the heart.

Whoever was hiding out there was a pretty good shot. Probably had some training, like a certain ex-cop.

Grady Small would have laughed, if his shoulder hadn't hurt so much. He was going to be killed by one of the things he had learned to do right.

Lilah's driver got it next, shot in the meat of his thigh as he was trying to get behind the cover of his car. The shot wasn't fatal, but it brought him down. Lilah had taken cover as well, kneeling behind a stone bench. Her gun still pointed at the three demons.

David was waving his hands over his head. "Stop firing! Stop firing! We can still do the deal!"

What was that idiot up to? This whole plan had already gone down the toilet. Small had been brought to this party by a raving lunatic.

But David's shouting seemed to have done the trick. The sniper was silent. Only Lilah held a gun. The others watched her, unmoving.

"What are you trying to pull here, David?" Lilah demanded.

"Oh, I think it's just about done. We've got to wait a minute for the final piece of the puzzle to join us. But then I think you're going on a trip with our friends here."

Lilah stared at him in shock. "Wolfram and Hart will have your hide."

He grinned as he sauntered over to her. "Why should I care? Let's say I got a better offer." He exhaled a ball of crystalline mist that enveloped Lilah for an instant before it disappeared. She jumped up in surprise, trying to wave the sparkling cloud away.

Gunn came up behind her and knocked the pistol from her hand.

"The real David's long gone," said the demon wearing David's body. "Tried to set up a meeting with the Seven Sinners. Can you imagine? Good riddance, is all I say. His knowledge and connections, though, especially concerning the security systems of his former employer, have been very helpful."

Lilah looked very angry. She crouched slightly, her hands open before her, like she knew how to fight. "Keep away from me!"

The demon Gunn grabbed Lilah from behind as the one that looked like Phil grabbed her legs. The two of them threw her in the van.

"I think you need to go see your lover boy at the hotel," David said as they slammed the door shut behind her. "Of course, the Stone's there, too. It will all be over soon."

Small saw his demon double stride through the front entryway of the new office building.

"Took you long enough, didn't it?" David asked. "Fred drives, Gunn and Phil keep our guest company. You and I need to get one more soul into the mix—say, the soul of a senior partner?"

"Not so fast, asshole," Small's double replied. "I've got unfinished business."

"Well, of course. You and I are going to need all the energy we've got in the next couple of hours. I understand the Remorse can be very strenuous."

His demon double shook his head and walked toward Grady Small. "God, be glad you don't have to listen to that jerk any longer."

Small still had his gun! He had been watching all of this in a daze and hadn't even thought about shooting his way out of there. His .38 was still in his shoulder holster. He had to reach it with his bad arm. His shoulder was on fire. He touched the gun. The metal felt cool under his fingers. He tried to pull it free from the holster, but he couldn't grip the handle. His fingers had no strength.

A shadow fell over him. He looked up to see his other self looking down.

"Say good night, Grady," the demon said with a smile.

His double shot him point-blank.

He was too clever for all of them. The Sinner who wore the form of David Marsh would bring in the final player in their little game, and the Remorse would begin. "What need did they have for Angelus, when he could lead the way to victory?

He waited for the light to fade as his fellow Sinner bathed himself in the death of the real Grady Small.

"Come on. We have one more double to make."

The only Grady Small still alive fell into step beside him. "You're just going to march right in there and take one of these guys?"

David nodded. "Right under their noses. It's easy once you know all the security codes. We'll copy the senior partner as soon as we gain access to the top floor. Then I'll need you to escort the partner to the hotel, so that we might dispose of him properly."

"And how are you gonna do that?"

David pulled a small box from his pocket. "When I press this, every security camera in the place goes down. Follow me."

David led Small through an emergency fire exit that was never supposed to be opened from the outside, then down a series of empty service corridors to a waiting elevator.

"It's almost like we're the only people in the building," Small said nervously, barely above a whisper.

"We're the only people who matter," David agreed, "and we're not even human."

He inserted a key into the very top button after both of them had entered the elevator. He turned the key, the button lit. "This will take us right to the top."

The elevator doors closed, but the cage didn't move.

"What?" David jiggled the key back and forth.

And the elevator went away.

They stood in the middle of a large expanse, painted a blinding shade of white. They couldn't see where wall met floor or ceiling, or exactly what was the source of the near-blinding light.

"I think we've reached the top floor," Small said.

"Well, you've reached your destination," a high, clear voice replied. "But you're no longer at Wolfram and Hart."

A girl of about nine smiled up at them. She was dressed like a school girl from the nineteen-fifties, with long brown hair cut into bangs, a pretty red dress with a white collar, and Mary Jane shoes on her feet. David thought he'd never seen anything that looked so innocent.

"I think we're screwed," Small whispered at his side.

"I understand you're here to see the senior partners?" the girl asked politely. "Well, you can't talk to them directly. But you can talk to me." She smiled prettily. "The partners tell me you'd be wise to remove yourselves from this world immediately. Otherwise, they are quite certain you'll be destroyed."

David could sense that the actual partners were very close, as though they stood just behind the little girl. Their bodies might be hidden, but he could sense their essences, so close that he might reach out and take them. "We cannot leave without one of you," he replied. "You cannot stop the Remorse."

"On the contrary," the little girl said, still smiling. "You're not taking anybody here. It would make no difference anyway. You are destined for destruction."

David couldn't determine where the light came from, where the room ended, or where the senior partners really hid. It felt as though they had stepped out of the world, and into some other place, some place that even the Sinners had never seen before. They had a level of technology in this space barely even hinted at by the miracle machines in the regular, steel and glass building that housed the "real" Wolfram & Hart.

But David had a greater resource than technology. He held the power that had brought down a thousand worlds. The partners tried to hide their souls, but the Sinners had spent centuries ferreting them out. David felt as though he could touch them.

Their presence was faint, but he could feel it all around. They didn't realize how much power had filled the Sinners. Both David and Small had killed their doubles. They were now filled with the energy of death.

David reached deep inside and released his essence to surround the invisible force.

The little girl giggled. "Thank you, Sinner. That was exactly what we needed."

Something was wrong.

David couldn't move. He tried to shift his form, release his human shell, and return to the Stone. Nothing happened. "Help," he managed to croak.

"I'll get you out of here," said Small from behind him. He pulled out his gun. "Let him go! I'll shoot! And I'll keep on shooting until I hit you suckers!"

Would he shoot the little girl? But the little girl was gone.

Sinner Grady Small aimed past David's shoulder. He fired off a round. The bullet disappeared in the distance, with no sound of impact.

They couldn't see the walls, David realized, because there were no walls.

The little girl's voice boomed from nowhere, and everywhere. "At first, we were only going to give you a warning. But you would not listen. Now, we will have you witness your own destruction. Look behind you, Mr. Grady Small."

A door opened in the middle of whiteness.

The other Grady Small stepped through.

"I'm still alive, you mothers!" he yelled, pulling his gun from his holster.

"That's impossible!" his demon double shouted back. "I capped this guy between the eyes, from three feet away. No way this guy can be walking around."

"Nothing more than flesh wounds!" The real Grady Small had a gaping hole in his shoulder, surrounded by dried blood, and another gore-ringed hole right between the eyes. "No one beats Grady Small!"

"But he died!" the Sinner Small screamed. "I was filled with his power!"

"And do you feel his power anymore?" the girl's voice asked.

The demon Small turned his gun on his reborn double. He fired off a single round.

The bullet smashed the original's other shoulder.

"I don't feel a thing," the first Grady Small said with a smile. "But you will."

He shot the demon double four times. The other Grady Small exploded, splattering skin and bone and shards of stone, all of it evaporating in the too-bright air.

The real Grady Small turned toward David. "Should I shoot this one, too?"

The little girl had reappeared, smiling, at his side.

"If you wish," she said cheerfully. "But only once or twice."

Small fired two bullets into David's chest. The metal punctured his skin, burned in his chest, but he did not explode. Everything was held in check by the senior partners.

"Does it make you feel better?" the girl said to the large man at her side.

Small nodded. "It makes me feel damn good."

She nodded in return. "We always try to reward loyal employees." She waved at the frozen Sinner before her.

"And now to this thing that mimics David Marsh." She frowned for a moment, then continued. "From what the senior partners understand of your methodology, the essence of the demon who mimicked Grady Small will return to the Stone, though greatly diminished." She looked sadly up at

David. "I'm sorry, but your essence will be destroyed."

She smiled again. "It is the beginning of your Remorse, but the end for the Sinners. After this, you will not cross Wolfram & Hart. You, alas, will be no more. But the remaining demons will know not to confront us in any dimensions that we do business. Now you will have to excuse us. We have to plan for the real apocalypse. You have wasted quite enough of our time." She waved good-bye.

He was fading. Whoever controlled this place let the other David look down at his hands. He could see the white light shining through his fingers.

The girl had turned her attention elsewhere. "And as for you, Mr. Small, perhaps we'll be able to reinstate you."

Small looked down at the holes in his clothing. "But I've been shot." His hands ran across the dry, empty holes to either side of his chest, then warily touched the hole between his eyes. "I'm dead, aren't I?"

"True," the girl replied. "Most unfortunate. We do appreciate your sacrifice. But look on the bright side: You may even get a promotion."

Sound was fading. David was almost gone.

"Well, I always thought I joined Wolfram and Hart to get ahead. This wasn't exactly in my plans."

The dead Grady Small grew hazy in David's vision.

"We have a different set of rules here, after all," he heard the girl's voice say. "A somewhat longer career path. Don't worry, Mr. Small. We'll keep you in our files."

The light was fading. And the Sinner's part in it was fading too.

He had always been a part of the Great Remorse. The Seven Sinners did not die.

The Remorse had failed twice, in perhaps, a thousand dimensions. They had taken their Stone and fled to a new world. But, while weakened, they had always been together, always ready to grow strong again and reap the guilt of some new world.

What would they do without him? He had thought the quest would last forever. Would a new Seventh Sinner take his place?

This David Marsh would be the last form he would ever take.

Is this what the Seven Sinners had done to all those souls? Was this what it meant to die?

No more the warmth of the Stone, no longer part of the Great Remorse.

The voices were fading now. He heard laughter, but it was not his laughter.

There was nothing.

Not even darkness.

There was only the end.

CHAPTER SEVENTEEN

They had tied Lilah's hands and feet. She was left on the bare floor in back of the van to jostle and roll around with every bump and twist and turn. Apparently they wanted to keep her alive, but weren't too concerned about what condition she was in. The Sinners Phil, Fred, and Gunn rode in the cab up front. She could hear their voices through a small window that connected the compartments, but only when the van was moving slowly or had come to a stop. When the van was moving quickly, which was most of the time, the sound of the wheels on the road drowned out everything else.

The van made a sharp left turn. She rolled hard against the right wall of the van and felt a quick, burning pain. Her arm had been raked across a sharp metal edge. She rolled away and looked at the spot. A bit of metal twisted away from the van's frame where it joined the door.

She braced her feet against the grooves on the floor of the van and pushed her back against the side of the van, feeling for the jagged piece. The sharp metal edge poked her thumb. She didn't care. She just needed to shift a bit to get both hands up against the metal edge.

She moved her wrists up and down, working the ropes against the jagged edge. It took time, the van's twists and turns forcing her to roll away from her only hope of salvation. But she forced herself back into position, scraping rope against metal again and again, until the bonds on her hands frayed enough that she could pull her hands free.

She sat against the wall of the van, pulling her knees up, and started to pick at the knots that bound her feet. She had been trapped and helpless in this van for too long.

She had to get away from there before her double came to end her life.

The van stopped abruptly. Lilah rocked back toward the cab, hitting her head on the forward wall. She could hear her three captors talking up front. She curled back into a position that resembled the one she held when she had been tied hand and foot.

"Gone."

"Gone?"

"That's not possible."

"We have to go."

"What about—"

"Leave her here. She's tied. If we don't, we are all gone. "

She heard both doors slam up front. The three kept on talking, though she could no longer make out the words. A moment later, their voices faded to silence.

She pulled the last of the rope from around her feet and pushed herself forward into a crouch. She winced. She had at least a dozen bumps and scrapes, and she might have bruised a couple of ribs, but nothing felt really sprained or broken. She had been very lucky. Now she hoped her luck would hold out long enough for her to get away from there.

She tried the door. It swung open. The Sinners hadn't even bothered to lock it.

These demons were a little too sure of themselves. Maybe Lilah could figure out a way to use that.

She climbed out of the van and took a moment to stretch as she surveyed her surroundings. She knew exactly where she was. The van was parked around the corner from Angel's hotel.

Inside the cab of the van she saw her purse. She pulled open the door in front and grabbed it. It felt much too light. She looked inside and discovered the demons had discarded her cell phone and her wallet. They had only kept her gun.

Well, Lilah had a use for the gun too. She grabbed her purse and took a clumsy step away from the van. She might be all right, but somewhere in all of this she'd broken the heel of one of her shoes.

Well, that clinched it. She took off both her heels and walked barefoot across the street toward the Hyperion Hotel. Any port in the storm, she thought. She just hoped she wasn't walking into even greater danger.

The Sinners knew pain.

Danger!

They had lost one of their own. It had been very long, more than five hundred feedings on five hundred worlds, since they had last lost one of the Seven.

They had to gather now to heal. Once one of them was lost, it hurt them more each moment they had to wait. They had to make the Seven whole again.

It could be the ending!

Before this began, they had easily disposed of the elderly couple who'd lived in an apartment within view of the Hyperion Hotel. Before this loss, they had thought it would make a good final nest for them to rest the Stone of Remorse.

But this place would no longer serve. Though

they had added the energy of two new victims, they did not have enough.

One of the victims had returned from death, to challenge the energy.

That had never happened in all of the Remorse.

We could be no more!

He who had won then lost flailed within the web of the Seven, trying to retain that which he had been. But that was never the way. His negative thoughts must be removed. These human memories could be stubborn, but the Seven always moved on so that they might achieve their glory.

When we are Seven, we succeed.

They had been warned away from this world, but it was too late to change their ways. They would be too far diminished. It would take them far too long to rebuild their strength if they were forced to begin again. They needed the seventh part of their self to feel whole. They had to use great energy to bring the seventh.

And when they used great energy, it brought to them a great hunger. A hunger that could not wait.

They needed to feed upon all those who would serve the Remorse. They were waiting for them, all but one in place.

No one has ever stopped us before.

They had to overwhelm their victims now, feed upon death after death, to regain their full strength and fulfill their destiny.

Our thoughts are chaotic, even in union.

They had the imprint of too many souls. Those who held Lilah had to return; and those who had taken up their secret positions, all had to be brought together.

The seventh had to be reborn.

All have to give of themselves.

They would grow strong again with time.

There must be seven.

Now.

The final battle must begin.

Wesley had seldom seen so abrupt a change. One minute, the hotel was an oasis of calm, one man surrounded by his books.

In the next minute, the entire world crashed through the doors.

Fred and Cordy were first, with Connor between them, looking a little dazed.

"They've got Connor!"

"Pardon?"

"The demons got to him!" Fred explained. "They've gotten to everyone!"

"Not everyone. Just most of us." Wesley hoped reason would have a calming effect. By his reckoning, Angel, Cordy, and Lorne were still untouched.

"And they killed Phil," Cordy added.

"I am sorry to hear that." The few times they had worked together, Wesley had always found Phil a most agreeable fellow. "He seemed like a good soul."

Angel and Gunn stormed in next.

"Nothing. Nada. Bupkis," were Angel's first words.

"They moved the Stone," Gunn translated. "We got zip."

Lorne strode in, smiling, from the other room. "Well, at least we're one big happy family."

Wesley sighed. "They've duplicated a number of us, true. But we are still here, and we are still alive. We'll find a way to beat these demons yet. Four of us have a demon counterpart. We don't know about the other three. From what I understand, at least one's involved with something at Wolfram and Hart."

"Where you have a contact," Gunn pointed out.

"Who will call me as soon as there are any developments."

"He's right," Fred piped up. "They can't destroy us if we stick together."

"So we wait," Angel agreed. "What will their next step be?"

"Well, the Stone's no longer at that warehouse," Gunn said. "These creeps are going to have to find someplace else to put it."

"And I think it's going to be someplace close to us," Wesley added. "Maybe even inside the hotel."

Fred nodded. "Phil said something just like that, before they got him."

"Our doubles probably know enough about this place to sneak in." Gunn shook his head. "Heck, they've already snuck in."

"So we make a quick sweep of all the likely hiding places," Angel continued. "In pairs, people. And we wait for some attempt by these guys to draw us out. They can't do anything without us. Maybe that's their real weakness. They need us. They want to ambush us, get the advantage. We're not going to let that happen."

"In the meantime, I think we need to get a little sleep." Wesley nodded to Fred and Gunn, who both looked exhausted. "These things drain your energy. We'll nap in shifts. We'll need all the strength we've got when they come after us again."

Wesley looked up from his reading. Night had fallen. How had all that time gone by?

Someone was rapping on the front door.

He got up from his desk to get a better view. "Lilah?" He quickly climbed the steps and unlocked the front door. "What are you doing here?"

She looked a little worse for wear. Her tailored suit was wrinkled and torn at the shoulder. Her hair was knotted and disheveled. She shifted back and forth on filthy feet.

"Are you all right?" he asked.

"I've been better," she replied. "Don't you usually keep this door open to encourage clients?"

"Yes, but only when we aren't surrounded by murderous, soul-devouring demons."

"I see your point. I've just had a close encounter of the worst kind with these demons. They abandoned me in the back of a van parked just around the corner. I believe they've set up shop in your neighborhood."

She briefly explained her encounter with the demons on the plaza, and how her assistant had revealed that he was a demon as well.

Wesley nodded. "And what happened to your assistant and this Small fellow?"

"I believe they went off to see the senior partners."

"And that would mean?"

"It was a mistake. Whatever plan they had, I'm quite certain the senior partners got the better of them. The partners have dealt with far worse than the Sinners."

Now that was an interesting statement. Not that Lilah would give him specifics about that sort of sweeping claim.

"It could be a setback for the Seven Sinners," Wesley replied. "Perhaps this would be a good time to strike, when they have been weakened. And you say they stopped in this neighborhood?"

"You can see the front of their van if you look out the door."

"I think we need to get the rest of my associates

here to proceed with this. You may have to repeat parts of your story."

"As long as I have someplace to sit. This hasn't been my best day."

"And I think it's far from over."

So this, Lilah thought, *is what the Spanish Inquisition felt like. Except those Inquisition victims probably had to suffer fewer baleful stares.*

Wesley had gathered the group together. Gunn and Fred sat on either side of her, encouraging her to keep her distance, she guessed, from those few at Angel Investigations who hadn't been contaminated. She told her story again: her betrayal by her assistant, her ride in the van, the sudden disappearance of her captors.

Gunn looked especially sour. "How do we know we can trust her? How do we know she's even who she says she is?"

"Well," Cordy suggested, "she could always sing."

"Yeah, it's probably time for all of us to sing." Gunn looked straight at Lilah. "You first."

Oh, yes. The fabled demon power of Lorne's. Well, if it would prove she was the real thing . . . she did far more embarrassing things back when she pledged a sorority. "Anything in particular?" she asked.

"Your choice," Lorne replied. "That always works best."

Lilah thought for a moment: The only song she

could remember was "Wake Me Up Before You Go-Go." It had meant something to her when she was six. She sang the first four lines a bit tentatively.

"I think she's the real thing," Lorne replied. "But there's something in there—"

Was he going to accuse her of something? Lilah looked back at the demon. "Wait a moment. Who checks on Lorne?"

"Pardon?" The green demon looked taken aback.

"Lorne checks all of us through our singing, to hear our voices and vouch that we're not our demon doubles," Lilah explained. "But who can check on Lorne?"

Lorne grinned at the others. "This is silly. I haven't even been out of the hotel."

"But the demons have already been in the hotel," Gunn replied. "Twice."

"I was working with Wesley."

Wesley shook his head. "We weren't together all the time." He glanced back down at his books. "I did find some tests in my research about telling demons apart. So we may have other methods." He smiled apologetically. "I'm afraid they involve leeches."

Lorne was looking a little frantic. "Campers! Are you suggesting the Seven have done the old switcheroo on yours truly? What would they want with a demon who was only visiting here anyways?"

Angel glanced at Wesley. "I think leeches are a great idea."

Lorne shrugged. "If you insist." He pirouetted across the floor, stopping a foot in front of Angel, and spat out a crystal cloud.

He stepped quickly away. "Well, we were waiting for a better time. Say, when all of you weren't in the same room together."

Gunn lunged for the demon, but he dodged the attack.

"It's those dance classes. They keep you nimble." He waved to Angel. "Welcome to the fold, old pal."

Faster than Lilah's eyes could follow, Angel jumped forward and grabbed the fake Lorne around the neck. He lifted the demon from the ground. "You don't think you're going to get away that easily?" Angel asked. "We'll need you to stick around and answer a few questions."

"Actually, I think not," the demon managed, despite the choke hold. The false Lorne pulled a short knife from inside his yellow jacket and promptly stabbed himself in the chest. He grimaced. "This is not . . . the most pleasant way . . . to travel."

Angel let go as Lorne transformed from scaly green to rock to molten goo. In an instant, he was gone.

Everyone stood for a moment in stunned silence. Lilah noticed that no one was thanking her.

"Get the number of that Greyhound bus!"

Lorne groped his way down the stairs from the second floor, a damp cloth pressed to his horned forehead.

"Man, why didn't anyone come look for me?" He stopped as he saw the startled look on everybody's faces. "Is everyone all right?"

Fred smiled. "Lorne. We're just glad you're okay."

"Just got a visit from your not-so-better half," Gunn added.

"I've got a demon double too?" Lorne asked. "I was afraid of that." He nodded to Wesley. "Maybe half an hour ago. You came up to the room to talk to me. Except it wasn't you. Before I knew it, it was icky-spray time. And then they knocked me out."

"You know what this means?" Wesley countered. "They don't have to make any more doubles. Everybody's in place."

"That's the good news?" Lorne asked.

"There's more of us than them," Connor piped up.

"So it's showdown time," Gunn said.

"More than that," Lorne agreed. "Time, I think, for the Gunfight at the OK Corral."

CHAPTER EIGHTEEN

The Remorse would be great.

The Seven had lost one of their own. So each gave of itself, so that Seven could be reborn. And Seven could take the lives they needed to begin the feeding they so desperately desired.

Seven of those they thought were in place. Six patterns had been placed upon the Sinners: Winifred Burkle, Charles Gunn, Wesley Wyndam-Pryce, Lilah Morgan, the boy Connor, the demon Lorne. All six of those who still were part of the Stone had given of themselves to fulfill the final pattern. They chanted together, to weave the web that reached across dimensions, to create the seventh member, so that they might be whole again. All the Sinners were diminished by what they gave, but their seventh member would take on the final pattern and lead them to the conquest of this world.

"He comes," one says for all.

"He comes," all say together.

"Bring him forth," one says for all.

"Bring him forth," all say together.

"He is the one," one says for all.

"He is the one," all say together.

"We are all one."

"We are all one."

"He is Angel."

"He is Angel."

A dark cloud formed in the recesses of the Stone. A cloud that at first had no form, but then took on color and shape, a near-human form and near-human features. This was the first time the Seven had ever captured a vampire, for Angel was the rare vampire with a soul. The cloud shifted and grew, blossoming forth out of the Stone of the Remorse, the insubstantial wisps of fog gaining depth and weight, first transforming to a moving pile of stone, then laying on the flesh disguise, giving the new sinner eyes and hands and mouth and brain, a near-perfect duplicate of the original. But this one was far better than a simple vampire with a soul. For this one had no thoughts of redemption. No thoughts for the safety of others. No wishes for peace and home. This copy wanted only to feed, to be bathed in the guilt of the Remorse. He, with all the Sinners, was driven by that single need, and would let nothing stop them from their goal.

The Sinners had devastated a hundred times a hundred worlds. The Sinners could not be defeated.

The last of the Sinners was made whole. He flexed his muscles, opened his eyes, and grinned at the six around him.

"Angel," one said.

"Angel," all but he repeated.

"Actually," the newest Sinner replied, "I'm feeling a bit more like Angelus."

"We wait for them to come to us," Angel announced. "They need us to ignite their apocalypse. We'll try to stay together as much as we can, while they'll try to draw us apart. We won't kill our own doubles at first—unless we have to in self-defense. It's after we force a couple of them back to the Stone that this gets interesting."

"They've brought the Stone quite close for the final battle," Wesley agreed. "And they may move it closer still."

"So they can attack us again and again," Gunn added. "Wear us down."

"I think, to be safe, that we need to destroy both them and their Stone."

"That would be rather final."

"But while each of us must kill their own double," Angel continued, "there's nothing to say, is there, Wes, that others can't help in their demon's demise?"

234

Wesley shook his head. "Nothing that I've seen."

"Nothing on our databases either," Lilah added.

"Fine. Then no matter what happens, we spend as much time together as possible. And we always work in teams."

"So what now?" Cordy asked. "Do we just sit here and wait?"

"I don't think we can keep them from getting in," Angel replied. "But we can reduce the element of surprise. I'd say we should post two sentries, Gunn and Connor, in the two opposite corner rooms on the third floor."

"That way we can see pretty much around the whole building," Gunn agreed.

"Right. Let's see where they're coming from. It will probably lead us a lot closer to the Stone."

"But wouldn't that leave both Gunn and Connor alone and exposed?" Wesley pointed out.

"Exactly!" Angel replied with a bit of a smile. Looked like he was trying to plan a bit too off-the-cuff. "So we send up sentry teams! Fred goes with Gunn, Cordy with Connor." He glanced over at his son. From the way the boy smiled, he could tell that Connor backed this part of the plan.

"You'll keep in touch with the lobby with your cell phones," Angel continued. "Lorne will handle the phones down on this end. If we get any of the demons to go sploosh down here, so they have to regenerate, we'll give you a heads up to look for them. Once we get a fix on the Stone, we bring it in and destroy all the Sinners." He grinned at his audience. "What could be simpler?"

"So we simply have to kill ourselves?" Lorne asked.

"Correct," Wesley agreed. "Phil thought that was so, and Lilah confirmed it from Wolfram and Hart's database.

"Remember," Wesley added after a moment, "the demon is a rather negative version of yourself. They will try to play on your guilt, exploit your weakness. By the time you're done listening to them, you'll be ready to kill."

Fred shook her head. "This news just gets better all the time."

"Wesley, Lilah, Lorne, you're all down here with me. For now, all of us stick to the lobby. And arm yourselves."

Lorne grabbed a crossbow, Connor a spear. Gunn had his ax, Cordy her short sword, and both Wesley and Lilah were carrying guns. And Angel? Well, he had his charm, good looks, and vampire strength and cunning. What more could he ask for?

"Any questions?" Angel asked. There were none.

"Well, let's move, people," he called. "It's going to be an interesting night."

"That depends on how you define 'interesting,'" Lorne said as he slid behind the desk. "I'd define it as a quiet night at Caritas, deep in conversation with a lovely two-headed Xerxel demon, a newly chilled bottle of champagne at your side. . . ."

He stopped talking when he realized no one was listening.

"So are you going to listen to me or not?" the demon Angel demanded.

The other Sinners shut up and looked at him.

"We're doing this under my command," the one who fancied himself Angelus continued. "I've known this hotel for better than fifty years. I have a history here." He smiled, showing his fangs. "When you're a vampire of the world, you get a history everywhere."

The Gunn and Connor demons started to argue at the back of the room.

"Hey!" Angelus demanded. "You don't listen to me, I stuff you back in the Stone, head first."

That shut them up.

"We need strength. We've been diminished by turning six into seven." He chuckled. "Gotta keep that magic number. If we're gonna succeed here, we're gonna have to make a couple of quick kills."

"I beg your pardon," Sinner Wesley spoke up angrily, "but we succeeded quite nicely before you arrived. We have all the major players in place, and the energy from our recent kills has kept us strong."

"Oh, really? Let's look at that success, shall we? You did manage, just barely, to include both sides of the apocalypse in the group of seven. But you've barely gotten a piece of Wolfram and Hart." He leered at the demon Lilah. "And who have you killed lately—some two-bit private eye, a cop on a hospital detail, an old couple because we needed their apartment. Come on, people! This isn't the kind of quality mayhem that brings on the Remorse! So you did get one minor functionary at W and H, good old Grady Small, before he came back from the dead and took back most of his energy. And look at your track record when you went after a major player. Those senior partners nearly trashed this whole party before we could even begin.

"Let's face it, people. Without me to guide you, you've been unable to bring down even one of the major stars of the apocalypse. It's a wonder we're even still in this game! But with me in control, we're going to get this thing done."

"And how soon are we gettin' down?" Not-Gunn demanded.

"This is going down tonight. Our strength is low. We need to build it up, now. I say we go in there and hit their weakest links, the most vulnerable of the Seven. We kill them, get their energy, bingo, we've got the strength to do in the rest."

"So who gets to die first?" Not-Lilah asked.

"Not you, dear," Angelus replied. "I think we should target one Goody Two-Shoes—Fred—and one demon lounge singer."

Both the doubles shifted in their seats, as though angry for being singled out.

"We'll leave this place in ones and twos. Spread out so it's harder for them to tell where we're coming from. Later, after a kill or two, when we've gained a little strength, we'll bring the Stone over to the hotel and do in the rest of them."

He smiled at the others. "I can't think of a classier place to hold an apocalypse than the Hyperion Hotel. Can you?"

CHAPTER NINETEEN

Lorne answered the ringing phone. "Movement in the east!" he reported. "Two people crossing the street. Looks like Gunn and Fred."

The phone rang again a few seconds later. "Movement in the west. One person, looks like Connor."

And again, less than a minute later. "Somebody's coming up on the south! Looks like Lilah and Wesley."

So they weren't going to get a fix on the Stone of Remorse. Angel realized he was fighting someone who thought an awful lot like himself.

A window crashed back toward the kitchen.

"Aren't they being a little obvious?" Wesley asked.

"It's where they want us to run," Lilah cautioned, "while the main force comes in through someplace else. But where would that be?"

"In this hotel? Down from the roof, up through the sewer tunnels. They could break into one of the old, boarded-up shops down along the far side of the hotel, or rebreak the back door that the Gunn demon came through before."

"We've fortified most of those weak spots, of course," Wesley added quickly, "but whatever extra barriers we've erected can still be broken down."

Lilah nodded. "The dark underside of a gloomy old hotel."

"Should we go investigate?" Wesley asked as he rose from his chair.

"Carefully," Angel replied. "I'd say you and Lilah could go a few steps down the back hall, listen for any noises. Our demon friends don't seem to particularly value being quiet."

"You don't need to bother about noise complaints if you're taking over the world," Lorne said.

"And if we do hear something?" Lilah asked.

"We take this battle one step, and one crash, at a time. And remember: We work in pairs!"

Fred watched the street to the east, while Gunn surveyed the alleyway to the south.

"I don't see anybody else coming. Do you?" Fred asked.

"What is it, too quiet for you?" answered an all-too-familiar voice behind her.

Fred spun to see her double.

241

"Little miss goody-goody," the demon said with a wicked smile. "Always wants to please everybody. Won't speak unless spoken to. Well, you don't need to hide anymore, because now it's time to die."

The Sinner shrieked as Charles buried the ax blade in her shoulder. "Why did you do that? Charles, I knew you never really loved me!"

"Oh my," Fred said.

Gunn shook his head. "Let's call it down, tell them we sent your double back. See if it comes back the same way as before. And Fred? Let's never argue, huh?"

He looked down as the last drops of the yellow liquid sizzled on the floor. While the slime stuck to human skin, it always ate away at other surfaces.

Charles shook his head. "We're going to have to replace the rugs in this place."

"And what are you doing back here?" Angelus asked.

The other Fred shook herself as she re-formed from the Stone of Remorse. "I wanted to surprise them! Quick in and out! Gunn wanted to case the place first. So I left him behind."

"So they popped you back here." Angelus wanted to pop her one himself. "You were lucky you weren't killed."

"By lovely little Winifred?" The demon laughed harshly. "Be real."

"Oh, I imagine Fred could kill even you, given enough opportunities. Now go back there and surprise her again! But this time go with Gunn."

The other Fred glared back at him, but stomped out the door.

Angelus shook his head. "I'm probably going to have to do all this myself."

"Fred's on her way again," Lorne relayed from the phone. "She's coming from the south."

"That's probably where they've stashed the Stone," Angel replied.

"In one of those nice old apartment buildings over there? I thought they were all occupied."

"They were," Angel agreed. "Until the Sinners showed up. The demons probably wanted a place with easy access—either going to be a first floor or a basement."

"We haven't seen your demon half yet, have we?" Lorne asked. "Or mine?"

"I'm thinking one of them's probably guarding the Stone," Angel replied. "I'm sure we'll see both of them soon enough."

A tremendous crash came from the kitchen.

"Oh, this is too much!" Wesley's voice came from down the hall. "They're tearing this place apart."

"Don't let them draw you in!" Angel ordered. There was no response. He swore softly. "Lorne!" he called. "Follow me."

The green demon came out from behind the desk.

"I need you to stay in the lobby," Angel explained, "but come over by the back hall to the kitchen. I'm going down there to check on Wesley and Lilah. Call out if anything happens."

"Anything?" Lorne asked.

"Anything," Angel replied. Then he was gone. Sometimes, Lorne wished vampires weren't so darned fast.

Well, Angel was just down the corridor. He had the cell phone to call the people upstairs. He had his trusty crossbow at his side. He had this large lobby all to himself.

No, he didn't.

"Now *this* is show business!"

The Sinner Lorne stood just inside the front door.

"Isn't it nice we can have this little chat?" The other Lorne smiled as he smoothly shuffled down the front stairs. "Seeing as how our interests are so much more refined than the others'."

The real Lorne realized that, although he had the crossbow in his hands, he hadn't bothered to load the bolt. He might have to distract the other fellow for a little bit while he prepared. "I'm sorry," he called out to the Sinner Lorne. "But have we been introduced?"

"Very funny," the demon double replied. "But

then, comedy always was one of our strengths. That helps when you're always running away from things, doesn't it? Like your family on your home-world, the wreck you made of Caritas, even this place for a while when you fled to Las Vegas." The double reached inside its yellow coat and pulled out a nasty-looking knife. "And then there's that high-girlie singing voice of yours. So appropriate when you scream."

Lorne's hands shook as he tried to load the cross-bow. He had thought all these things, too, but he knew they weren't true. "Oh, fellows?" he called over his shoulder. "Angel? Wesley? Lilah?"

He was answered by another crash from the kitchen.

Wesley couldn't help himself. He had to get a look at this.

"Do you think you could make any more noise to bring them down on us?" the demon Lilah spoke icily to her partner.

"You don't approve of good old breaking and entering?" the demon Wesley replied with a sneer. "Why don't you use some of your Wolfram and Hart super-science instead?"

This had apparently been going on for a while.

He turned back to Lilah, who stood just behind him. "We're like an old, bickering married couple," he whispered.

Lilah nodded. "Remind us not to stay together for twenty years."

Connor, or somebody who looked just like him, jumped from behind the stove, screaming like a banshee. Wesley barely ducked a sizable saucepan that came flying through the air.

This was the real ambush. And he'd walked right into it.

The demon Connor came screeching for them, with the other demons close behind. Lilah had her gun in hand. Her demon double ducked back behind a sink. She shot the demon Wesley instead. He made a high-pitched cry, clutching at his chest as he turned from flesh to stone to the usual goo.

Wesley had his hands full with Connor. The demon boy was throwing everything he could get his hands on, no doubt attempting to distract the real Wesley until his demon double could sweep in for the kill.

"Enough!"

This Connor might be as fast as the original, but Angel was even faster. Angel leaped past Wesley and grabbed the demon that looked like his son. The Connor thing wriggled from his grasp. Angel got it by the throat. The false Connor wildly flung itself away, landing in a mass of kitchen knives. The demon grabbed a large cleaver and spun back to face Angel. Angel lashed out with his foot, trying to knock the blade away. The Connor thing tried to turn away from the blow, the heel of Angel's shoe knocking the hand with the cleaver up against the demon's chest. The sharp blade cut through cloth and what doubled for flesh. The Connor thing cried out once.

The demon turned to mush like all the others.

Angel looked at the hand that had held the demon's throat. "That's something I didn't enjoy."

"That was only the image of your son, Angel." Wesley didn't know how they could ever resolve their tortured past.

Lilah glanced over at Wesley, while still keeping her gun ready for any movement in the kitchen. "I didn't know you could scream that high."

"Me?" Wesley sounded a bit offended. "That was the demon you heard, Lilah."

Lilah only smiled.

"But we didn't kill your double," Wesley reminded her. "And it looks like she left the premises."

Lilah nodded. "She's out there somewhere, waiting for me." She waved her gun at the kitchen. "But I'm waiting for her, too."

Wesley stepped cautiously into the kitchen, his own gun drawn, glancing down at the last remaining bits of the two Sinners. "Well, that's certainly a mess."

Angel turned back toward the lobby. "Did you hear something from Lorne?"

• • •

Nobody answered Lorne's pleas.

"Do you think anybody really wants to help you?" his double asked sarcastically. "They just keep you around for a laugh. Oh, they do find you useful occasionally. Sort of like a caged bird, good for the special song."

Lorne still couldn't get the bolt to fit. Why hadn't he practiced with this thing some more? The demon double was quickly crossing the lobby. If it was going to kill Lorne with that knife, it would need to get in close.

Lorne held the crossbow like a club. Perhaps he could keep his double at arm's length for a bit. But he needed a better weapon.

The double lunged for him as Lorne grabbed the heavy lamp from the nearby table. He jumped back. The knife didn't even graze him. He brought the lamp down, hard, on the head of his assailant.

That was a nice thing about these old hotels. They always had those good, solid lamps.

The demon double sank to the floor, a sizable dent in its skull. It went into a sudden series of violent spasms, screaming a single, clear, high note.

Then it burst into flame.

"Well, that was certainly different."

Angel stood behind him. Wesley and Lilah stepped out of the hallway.

"I appear to have killed my double," Lorne admitted.

"As we all will have to do," Wesley agreed.

"Well I know you were trying to locate the Stone—"

"No," Angel replied, "we've sent enough of the others back. It's time to dispose of these things for good."

"Good," Lorne replied. "I always wanted to kill a critic."

CHAPTER TWENTY

This was all wrong.

They hadn't gotten close to Fred. And now the demons Wesley and Connor had both reappeared within the Stone with nothing to show for it.

Angelus was not pleased.

"What, am I working with the Seven Sinners here, or the Seven Stupids?"

The Wesley and Connor demons looked sullen, but had no reply. They would have to change their strategy. The Sinners would have to draw them out.

The Stone of Remorse sparked suddenly, then gave off the slightest of noises, like the wind through the trees.

The three Sinners looked to one another. They had lost another. One of their number had been killed by the one it had copied. Angelus closed his eyes and reached through the Stone to touch his fellows of sin.

The Sinner Lorne was no more. Lorne?

It didn't matter how it had happened. The six had already made a seventh. Without another death to fuel their creation. They didn't have enough energy to replace him.

"We could take the Stone," the demon Wesley simpered. "Leave this place. Find a new world for the Remorse."

"Too late," Angelus replied. "We have reached the endgame. We need to kill them all, and kill them quickly."

Angelus knew of only one way to accomplish his goals. "We are taking the Stone to the hotel."

Connor jumped away from the window. Cordy had to see this. "Look, Cordy! Out on the street! They're bringing the Stone here!"

Cordy came to stand close beside him. He pointed down to the broad avenue below, where demons who looked like Wesley and Connor carried a very heavy object between them.

"That's the Stone?" Cordy asked in disbelief.

"I guess so," Connor answered. "What else could it be?"

"It's just so . . . stone-like. I guess I was looking for more of the sparkling diamond sort of thing." She shrugged. "Evil jewels seem more appropriate for destroying the world." She reached for her cell phone. "We'd better let Angel know about this."

But Connor was already on the move. "My double's down there, lugging that rock," he called over his shoulder. "I can get rid of him, just like that."

He ignored her calls to come back. Sure, Cordy was worried about him. But he'd show her what a real hero could do.

Lorne had thought that going back to answering the phones would make things less complicated. "That was Cordy," he said to Angel as he put down the phone. "Apparently, the Sinners are bringing the Stone of Remorse to the hotel."

"Well, that makes our life easier," Angel replied.

Lorne let the other shoe drop. "Connor's gone out by himself, to stop them."

"Well, that doesn't."

Angel headed for the door.

Connor rushed out to the broad avenue he had seen from upstairs. The two demons had brought the large rock up onto the sidewalk directly in front of the hotel.

A voice spoke from the shadows:

"Drop the Stone." The voice's owner stepped into the light. It looked like Angel, but Connor knew it wasn't.

"Drop the Stone," the demon repeated, "and finish your business."

The two demons did as they were told. The one who looked like Wesley retreated into the shadows. The one who looked like Connor swaggered forward with a smile.

"You think you're going to kill me?" the false Connor taunted. "What do you know? What do you know about anything? What have you done since you've come to this world? Maybe you could have saved your father."

"What do you know about that?" Connor called.

"I know as much as you do, maybe more." The Not-Connor laughed. "Maybe he was never your father at all."

Connor's next reply died in his throat. He couldn't let this creature goad him. You control your emotions if you want to survive. It was a lesson his father had taught him well.

"Who is your father, anyway? Maybe nobody is your father! Maybe your every thought is a lie."

The creature was trying to drive him crazy.

"Maybe you don't even deserve to live." The demon flashed a nasty-looking knife.

But Connor still had his spear. He stepped away as his double rushed in, knocking aside the attack with the shaft of his spear.

"Pretty fancy moves, vampire boy." His double was still smiling. "You want a piece of me?"

Connor shifted the spear in his hands. He was sure his double wanted to get him to throw it in anger and lose his advantage. Instead, he walked forward slowly, jabbing his spear at his opponent.

The demon knocked the spear aside for an instant and jumped toward Connor. But Connor was ready for the move. He rolled away, twisting around so that he came back up on his feet. The demon leaped for him, knife slashing the air. Connor ducked beneath the blow, driving his spear up in the air at the same time.

It caught the demon Connor in the throat, and passed clear out below the base of his skull. The demon hung there for an instant, writhing and screaming.

"Who deserves to live now?" Connor asked quietly.

The demon burst into flames on the end of his spear.

It was only when she sat down that she realized how exhausted she was.

Lilah realized she had been through a lot in the last few hours—an aborted takeover of Wolfram & Hart, her abduction and mistreatment in the back of a van, her escape to the relative sanctity of Angel Investigations, and now a battle for her soul. Not that her soul hadn't already been claimed by others. She still wanted some say in its final destination.

The others had gone out on the street. Lilah was too tired to move.

She opened her eyes. A voice whispered to her from the shadows:

"Lilah, maybe we can make a deal."

She realized it was her own voice talking, but it was her voice coming from a demon.

"You're good at making deals, aren't you?" the voice went on. "Always getting by—more than getting by, really, always coming out on top. Why do you need the petty concerns of this world? I can show you worlds and worlds of pain."

Her gun was back in her purse. She covered it with her hand. She stood up slowly. "What do you mean? What are you offering me?"

"A world beyond guilt. A world beyond tears. The Seven Sinners need your strength. Why do you need a petty job in a petty law firm? Come with us, and you will rule whole worlds."

Lilah turned casually toward the voice. She could just barely make out a figure standing in the shadows. "You say this, but how can I trust you?"

"You know how desperate we are. Our numbers are diminished, our power nearly gone. We must recruit new souls to fill the void, souls that are already corrupt. You are the only true candidate here. Accept, and you will live forever."

"And if I have second thoughts?" Lilah asked.

The demon Lilah jumped from her hiding place, a cleaver from the kitchen in her hand.

Lilah shot her four times.

The demon fell back against the wall, her body twitching for an instant. The creature screamed as its body was engulfed in flame.

"You were right about one thing," Lilah replied to the burning corpse. "I always come out on top."

No demon could beat her. Especially not a so-called Sinner. Lilah's guilt was buried so deep, no one would ever find it.

"Now we're gonna finish what we started."

Fred recognized Gunn's voice.

The Charles Gunn by her side, the real Gunn, turned to the door. His double, and Fred's double, stood there side by side.

"We didn't start anything," the real Gunn said to the newcomers. "But we'll be glad to finish it."

Fred was never big on killing. But this was their lives they were talking about here, and maybe the lives of the whole world. And these demons had killed Phil—one of the nicest guys she had ever met, before or after her unscheduled stay in a demon dimension.

They should work as a team. That's what Angel had said.

Charles held the ax he'd been favoring for the past few days. Fred, unable to decide, had brought up a half dozen knives and a small hatchet for protection. Now she had to use them—one of them, at least.

"Stick close to me, babe," Charles said. He was the one with experience. He should take the lead.

The demon Gunn stepped into the room first too. He carried a sword.

"Oh, look at the size of that ax you're handling, man!" the demon called. "Trying to make up for some lack in your manhood?"

Sparks flew as sword and ax struck each other: once, twice, then a third time. Each Gunn knew how the other one moved. Fred wondered how she could swing the battle back her way. "Oh, Charles," she crooned, in that deep voice she knew he liked. "Maybe that's what I need. Why would I want you when I could get a demon lover?"

The demon grinned at that. "Yeah, babe. Two on one. Now we're talking."

Fred pulled up her skirt. The other Charles's gaze followed the motion.

And the real Charles lopped off the demon's head.

The Fred demon screamed, running forward with a long kitchen knife. The real Fred flung the hatchet across the room. It caught the demon between the eyes.

The remains of both demons fell to the floor.

"A demon lover?" Charles asked.

"Hey," Fred replied. "I know you always like it when I talk dirty."

They held each other as the demons burned and died.

When all else failed, Wesley returned to the printed page. He hoped he could find the best way to destroy the Stone.

"Why do you bother with any of this?" his voice said from across the lobby. "These people who don't appreciate you? The woman, Lilah?"

The demon Wesley smiled as he sauntered forward. "You don't think you've ever really satisfied her? She's just using you. That's all that women ever really get out of you. Never any commitment. Never any love."

Wesley stood up. "I've been down that path before. And I realize it isn't true."

"Besides," Lorne's voice came from the office, "you didn't think you'd find Wesley alone out here, did you?" He walked into the lobby, loaded crossbow in hand.

Lilah stepped from the corridor leading to the kitchen. "After all, we've already disposed of our doubles. Shouldn't we give Wesley a hand in killing his?"

The Wesley demon's head swung back and forth, like some trapped animal. "So you're going to let your friends kill me? I'll come back, over and over again!"

"Not if I do this." Wesley pulled out his gun and shot his double in the heart.

The demon fell and burned.

"Do I really look that pitiful?"

Lilah shook her head. "Not so much lately."

Wesley looked to Lorne. "We have to help Angel. Call the others. We're going after the Stone."

CHAPTER TWENTY-ONE

"No!" the demon Angel cried out as he watched the demon Connor burn. "I will not let it end like this! I will kill you all!"

"So you call yourself Angelus?" The real Angel stood before him.

"I am Angelus. And I am your death."

"I don't think so." Angel looked to either side of him. One by one, the others were coming out of the hotel.

"One more demon," Gunn said casually. "One more chance to kick some demon butt."

"You're only one demon out of seven," Fred pointed out. "And now the other six are gone."

"I'll kill all of you for sport!" Angelus called. "And then bide my time, until the Stone of Remorse brings the Sinners back, greater than before!"

"You call yourself Angelus, don't you?" Wesley asked.

"What better name?"

"But you're really just a twisted bit of Angel," the ex-Watcher explained. "You exist because you stole a tiny piece of Angel's soul."

"Hey," the real Angel said with a grin. "I've known that evil vampire for many, many years, and you, sir, are no Angelus."

The demon who called itself Angelus hissed at the crowd. "Enough of this talk! The Remorse never fails! I will have my revenge!"

He ran forward with a roar, heading straight for Fred.

But Angel was in his path in an instant, and drove a stake through his heart.

The creature didn't die like a vampire. The other Angel burned like all the demons before him.

"Do I ever get that melodramatic?" Angel asked.

"Not that much lately," Wesley replied. "But we have one more bit of business." He pointed to the Stone sitting on the sidewalk.

"And what do we do with it?"

"According to my research, smashing it would be sufficient."

Gunn looked down at the rock. "Wow. What's that gonna take?"

"Surprisingly little," Wesley said. "One well-placed blow in the very middle, by someone, say, with the strength of a vampire?"

"Hey, Gunn." Angel smiled. "Mind if I borrow your ax?"

Gunn handed him the large, two-bladed weapon. Angel walked to the Stone, raising the ax high above his head. He brought it down with all the force in his body.

The Stone shattered in a thousand tiny pieces, giving off a single, great groan—as if all the guilt locked inside it had been released forever.

"Well, another good night's work, wouldn't you say, kiddies?" Lorne asked from where he was standing in the doorway to the hotel.

Fred looked up the street. "All this noise we've been making. Won't the cops come down here?"

"Maybe," Gunn answered. "But what's for them to see? A few ashes, some broken bits of rock."

"The end of the Remorse," Wesley added.

Lilah came up to his side. "Time for me to go. Now that it's over, we have nothing in common. We're back to enemies again." She smiled at him. "Well, friendly enemies." She gave him a light kiss on the cheek.

"I've already called her a taxi," Cordy said.

"So we're done here?" Connor asked. It looked like he was also ready to leave.

"As done as we ever are," Angel replied.

The eight of them stood there for a long moment, and took in the quiet, guilt-free night.